STAR WARS®
GALAXY of FEAR

THE BRAIN SPIDERS

A real brain drain . . .

Zak and Tash followed Beidlo through a wide portal. "Take it from someone who spends every day trying to become one," Beidlo added. "There's absolutely nothing dark, mysterious, or wicked about the B'omarr monks."

As he said this, he led his visitors into an enormous room. Shelves lined the walls, but Zak's and Tash's eyes were drawn to a crowd of brown-robed monks standing around a table.

As soon as the newcomers entered, the monks whirled to face them. Angry eyes glared from beneath their hooded cloaks. One of the monks was holding something close to his body. Seeing what it was, Tash and Zak both gasped.

In his cupped hands, the monk held the squishy gray blob of a human brain.

Look for a preview of Star Wars: Galaxy of Fear #8, *The Swarm*, in the back of this book!

STAR WARS®
GALAXY of FEAR

BOOK 7

THE BRAIN SPIDERS

JOHN WHITMAN

BANTAM BOOKS
NEW YORK · TORONTO · LONDON · SYDNEY · AUCKLAND

To Kevin J. Anderson and Rebecca Moesta, for creating Hoole in the first place.

RL 6.0, 008–012

THE BRAIN SPIDERS

A Bantam Skylark Book / December 1997

ISBN 0-553-48637-3

Published simultaneously in the United States and Canada.

PRINTED IN THE UNITED STATES OF AMERICA
OPM 0 9 8 7 6 5 4 3 2 1

PROLOGUE

In the middle of a wide chamber sat a high table. A tray next to it was covered with sharp metal instruments.

On the table, a man struggled desperately, but his arms and legs were held down with unbreakable straps.

Several figures glided out of the shadows. One of them wore a long brown robe that hid his face.

"Is everything ready?" he asked.

Another nodded. "We can begin."

The first figure pulled back the sleeves of his long brown robe and from the tray picked up a wicked-looking blade.

"Please," said the man on the table. "I didn't do anything. Let me go!"

The figure in the brown robe did not respond.

"I'm begging you," the man pleaded again. "I didn't do anything. Please don't hurt me!"

The dark figure smiled. "Hurt you? You don't understand. I am not going to hurt you. I am going to show you the mysteries of the universe." He held up the sharp blade, which had many jagged sawlike teeth, and nodded to his companion. "All right, let's remove his brain."

CHAPTER 1

"Welcome to Koda Spaceport. Welcome—*zzzzz!* to Koda Spzzzzzz! port . . ."

The hospitality droid was programmed for one simple task—to welcome visitors to Koda Space Station. But one of those visitors had fired a blaster shot through the droid's main computer, frying its circuits. The tall, humanoid droid shuffled back and forth in the huge gateway, repeating his welcome over and over again.

Tash and Zak Arranda, along with their uncle Hoole, stood at the entrance to the spaceport.

"I can't believe no one's even bothered to fix him," Zak said sympathetically.

Tash looked past the droid into the passageway beyond. Blaster burns and scrawled graffiti covered the walls. Trash littered the floor. She couldn't tell exactly what kind of trash it was, but from the smell, she guessed it was old food, spilled drinks, and other things she didn't want to think about. "Looks like no one's bothered to fix a lot of things around here."

Hoole frowned. The lines on his long, gray face deepened. "I did not suspect Koda would be in such a state of disrepair. Still, it is a busy port, and a good place to hide. Let's proceed."

The tall Shi'ido led them past the shuffling droid and into the spaceport.

Koda was a tiny, insignificant spaceport in a small, backwater corner of the galaxy. The nearby planets were sparsely inhabited by a few poor settlements. The only people who came to Koda were local farmhands looking for excitement and bored smugglers looking for trouble.

"Stay close to me," Hoole ordered his niece and nephew.

Zak glanced back down the hall at the damaged droid. He sighed. "I miss Deevee."

Tash nodded. "I do, too. But he's happier now."

DV-9 had been their uncle's research droid. He had also been Tash and Zak's caretaker and friend. The droid had been heavily damaged during some recent adventures. They had been able to repair him, but Deevee told them, "I believe I've had all the excitement my servos can take."

Hoole had agreed to free the droid from service. It wasn't fair to keep dragging him around the galaxy—especially since they were still wanted by the Empire. With Tash and Zak's help, Hoole had been able to destroy a secret scientific experiment run by the Empire. Unfortunately, their victory had also made them a terrible enemy: Darth Vader. Zak, Tash, and Hoole had managed to escape his clutches, but now they were on the run, wanted in every star system in the galaxy.

All this was too much for the damaged droid. Deevee had retired to the Galactic Research Facility on the planet Koaan.

"I wish I was with Deevee now," Zak muttered as they waded through the trash-covered hallway.

"Oh, don't be such a baby," Tash said. "A little garbage won't kill you."

Tash saw her younger brother scowl at her. She shrugged. Lately, he'd seemed awfully immature to her. After all, she was thirteen heading toward fourteen—and he was only twelve, not even a true teenager yet.

"Anyway, we've been through worse," Tash went on confidently. "This place is nothing we can't handle. Right, Uncle Hoole?"

"Wrong."

Hoole had just stopped at the entrance to the spaceport's cantina. It was made of a hard, see-through material called transparisteel. On the far side of the entryway, they could hear screams, shouts, and laughter mixed with the sounds of glasses shattering and furniture smashing. Something—Tash couldn't tell if it was a very large person or a very large couch—banged into the transparisteel door like it had been thrown by a giant.

Zak started to speak. "It's like—"

"—the end of the world," Tash interrupted.

"Yeah," he agreed.

"No, look," she said, pointing at the sign on the door. "This place is *called* 'The End of the World.' "

"Aptly named," Hoole said. "This is the worst-run establishment I've ever seen. Even more dangerous than a cantina I once visited on Tatooine. I think you two should return to the ship."

"Why?" Tash objected.

Hoole turned his steady gaze on his niece. "Tash, I need to make sure there is no Imperial activity at this spaceport. I also need to decide what our next move will be. A cantina like this is the best place to acquire information. However, it is not the best place for children."

"Children!" Tash blurted out. "Uncle Hoole, we're not kids and we've been through worse than this."

Hoole paused. It was true. Tash and Zak had been through some frightening adventures. But all that was behind them now. There was no need to take unnecessary risks.

"Please return to the ship. I will meet you there

shortly," he said. Then he turned and walked into the End of the World.

"Okay by me," Zak said. "I'm about ready for things to get back to normal, anyway." He motioned to Tash. "What do you say we go back to the ship and play a few holo-games. I might even let you win at Starbattle!"

Tash frowned. "Hologames are for kids," she grumbled, and quickly followed Hoole into the noisy gloom of the cantina.

Tash blinked as her eyes adjusted to the darkness. She hadn't meant to snap at Zak like that—he was her best friend. But lately she'd started to feel, well, *older* than her brother. After all, she would be fourteen in a few weeks. Also, she had recently become aware of her sensitivity to the Force, the mysterious power used by the ancient Jedi Knights.

Squinting, Tash searched for Hoole, but the cantina was so dark that she could barely see where she was going. Besides, Hoole was a Shi'ido, and the Shi'ido were shape-changers. The moment he stepped into the dark bar, Hoole could have transformed into any shape in the galaxy.

The only real light leaked out of a row of tiny lamps over the squid-shaped head of the bartender. Tash saw many humans lined up at the bar, as well as a few alien species. There was a long-snouted Kubaz, a small group of pudgy Kitonaks, and a horn-headed Devaronian. But most of the customers seemed happier hiding in the shadows.

A bulky figure sitting at a nearby table suddenly let out a deep sigh, and Tash found herself engulfed in a cloud of smelly t'bac smoke.

"Hey!" she said without thinking. "You blew that smoke right in my face!"

She threw an angry glance in the direction of the smoker, and found herself looking into the ugliest face she had ever seen. One of the smoker's eyes was wide and bloodshot, but the other was so flat and squinty that it looked as if one side of his face had been crushed by a gravity well. His nose was wide and flat, and it bent in two different directions as it grew down from his forehead. His mouth was twisted into a permanent snarl. He had no neck—just two huge, sloping shoulders and a pair of arms thicker than Tash's waist.

"Yeah, I did," the smoker agreed with a growl. He blew another cloud of smoke that made Tash cough.

"Stop it!"

Slowly, the smoker stood up. He was almost as tall as a Wookiee. He leered down at Tash. "Who's going to make me, little girl?"

"I—" Tash swallowed. She knew she should just back off, but she hated being called *little girl*. "I will," she said weakly.

The bar fell silent. Everyone waited to see what the huge being would do.

The smoker looked at Tash again, then threw back his head and let loose a roar of laughter. Tash felt her cheeks burn with embarrassment. When the creature was done laughing, he put one huge hand on her head. Then he bent down to look her in the eye.

"Little girl, I would eat you for lunch if you were big enough to make a meal. You're lucky Drudo found me someone else to eat. Now run along before I decide to have an appetizer."

He spun Tash around so she was facing the opposite direction, then gave her a gentle shove that sent her stumbling across the dark cantina toward the exit. A ripple of laughter followed her.

When she regained her balance, Tash fumed. She didn't care how big that bully was—he didn't have the right to embarrass her.

She walked up to the bartender. "I want to see the owner."

The squid-headed bartender blubbered something in a thick, liquid-sounding language. It sounded like laughter. Then he said in Basic, "He's in the back room. But you don't want to disturb him. He's not in a very good mood."

"Yes, I do," Tash said stubbornly. The smoker had insulted her, but she decided to handle the situation like an adult. She would register a complaint with the management.

She strode over to a door next to the bar and stepped through as it slid open.

Tash found herself in a small, brightly lit room. A man in a white apron stood with his back to her, working over a table.

"Excuse me," she said.

"It's not ready!" the man yelled, whirling around.

As he did, Tash saw that the table was covered in blood. Then she looked at the man's hands. In one hand he held a blood-stained vibroblade. In the other he held a still-beating heart.

CHAPTER 2

The man stuck the throbbing heart in Tash's face and snapped, "Is this what you want?"

Tash jumped back in surprise and terror, trying to shut the horrible sight from her eyes and the smell from her nose. "No!" she shrieked.

The man blinked and looked at Tash again. "Wait a minute. You're not a Whiphid."

"No, I'm not," Tash said, her own heart pounding faster as the one in the stranger's hand began to slow. "I—I'm Tash."

The man grunted. "Sorry. Thought you were one of those Whiphid brats. There's a family of 'em in the cantina. Been pounding the tables asking for their meal for the last half hour." He jabbed his blade at the pile of guts on the table. "Whiphids are born hunters. Only like fresh meat."

Glancing at the table again, Tash realized that the blood and body parts belonged to a slaughtered nerf, not a sentient being. *Not that that makes things much better,* she thought, shuddering at the sight of the animal's remains. But at least she knew the manager wasn't some kind of mass murderer.

The man plopped the heart on the table and wiped his hand on his smock. "Name's Drudo. I run the End of the World. Wha'd'ya want?"

Tash took a deep breath. "I was in your cantina when a big man with a smashed face blew smoke at me. Then he threatened me. I want you to throw him out."

Drudo laughed almost as loudly as the bully had. He stabbed the blade down into the table so that it stuck there, quivering. "Big guy, you said? Smashed face? Was he about this tall?" Drudo stood on his tiptoes and stretched his hand up as high as he could.

"Yes, that's him," Tash replied. She felt more confident. This Drudo was treating her like an adult, and it looked like he was going to help her.

"Can't help ya," Drudo said.

"What?" Tash blurted. "Why not? You own this place, and I'm a customer. That man was rude to me!"

"Listen, kid," Drudo drawled. "You're lucky all he hurt was your ego. You got any idea who he is?"

Tash bristled at the word *kid,* and shook her head.

Drudo went on. "Well, I'll tell you. That there's Karkas, the most wanted criminal in about a hundred light-years.

12

He's got the death sentence in at least two dozen star systems. Everyone—and I mean *everyone*—wants that guy dead or behind bars. The Rebellion is after him, and so is the Empire. They say he's even wanted by a crime gang called Black Sun. You know how many people he's murdered?"

Again, Tash shook her head.

"Exactly ninety-one," Drudo said, glaring at Tash. "You know how I know?"

"How?" Tash asked.

"Because every time Karkas kills someone, he carves the letter *K* right on their forehead." The cantina owner drew the symbol in the air just millimeters from Tash's face. "Ninety-one times. Kid, that monster would swallow you whole and then forget he'd ever seen you. You're lucky to have walked away with your life."

"I agree," said Hoole.

Tash jumped. She hadn't seen or heard Hoole enter the room. He could be so quiet, sometimes she thought he floated across the floor.

Hoole put a hand on Tash's shoulder. "I believe I requested that you return to the ship for your own safety."

"Yes, but—" she started to say.

"I apologize for any inconvenience," Hoole said to the cantina owner.

Drudo picked up his knife and started hacking into the organs the Whiphids had ordered for lunch. "No problem. Not like she was keeping me from anything interesting."

Keeping one hand firmly on Tash's shoulder, Hoole escorted her quickly through the cantina and back down the hallway.

"Uncle Hoole, I could have taken care of myself," she insisted as they approached their ship.

"I doubt it," the Shi'ido said sternly. "This is a most dangerous place."

"If it's so dangerous, why did you bring us here?"

The slightest of frowns crossed Hoole's face. "An error. I was hoping to find someone with the skills to help us evade the Empire, but this place is too far out of the main space lanes. No one here has the equipment we need. We'll have to go somewhere else for help. Somewhere I had hoped never to visit again."

"Where?" Tash asked as they boarded the ship.

Hoole barely glanced at her. "To the palace of Jabba the Hutt."

An hour later the *Shroud* was traveling smoothly through hyperspace on its way to the planet of Tatooine. Zak and Tash had been there once before, when Hoole needed a favor from the gangster called Jabba the Hutt. But back then, Tash had been preoccupied with other troubles, and she hadn't paid much attention to the planet or its people.

That's because Uncle Hoole always seems to know where we're going, she thought. *He's always leading us around*

. . . like we were little kids. But I'll bet if I knew more about Tatooine, I could help him.

Activating the computer in her cabin, Tash called up information on the planet Tatooine. There wasn't much. It was a desert planet, a giant ball of dust spinning through space, with only a few small settlements and one busy spaceport called Mos Eisley.

"Still, there's got to be something unique about the place. Otherwise, why would Jabba the Hutt make his home there?" Tash asked herself.

She found a computer file that contained a detailed report on Tatooine. "Aha! I'll bet I can find something here Uncle Hoole doesn't know."

But her hopes were dashed when she saw who had written the report. It was Hoole! He had studied the planet years before and written an eyewitness account of its inhabitants. Tash knew that Hoole was an anthropologist and that it was his job to study different cultures. But there were so many mysteries surrounding her Shi'ido uncle that she'd nearly forgotten he had a job.

"He really *does* study people," she reminded herself. She skimmed the report, but read more closely when she found mention of a group of people called B'omarr monks. They seemed to be religious students, seeking knowledge and trying to understand the mysteries of the universe. Tash wondered if their studies included the Force. Tash was fascinated by the ancient Jedi Knights and the Force that gave

15

them their power. And even though she'd recently learned that the Force was with her, too, she had no one to teach her how to use it.

Now that I'm getting older, she thought, *I'll need a teacher. Maybe the B'omarr monks can help.*

Reading on, she smiled. Uncle Hoole had called his research work boring, but his report was filled with drama. On Tatooine, he had been chased by tribal savages called Sand People and had nearly been captured by Imperial stormtroopers. Wherever Uncle Hoole went, Tash thought, trouble seemed to follow.

ALERT! ALERT! ALERT!

Suddenly, the lights in her cabin went out, and the small red emergency light blinked as alarms blared in her ears. Tash leaped a full meter out of her seat.

That was the collision alert! They were going to crash!

Scrambling to her feet, Tash threw herself at the door. As it slid open, she stumbled out into the hallway to find . . .

. . . Zak, standing in the corridor, laughing hysterically.

There were no alarms in the hallway. No emergency lights.

No crash.

Just Zak, giggling and holding two wires that were connected to a panel in the wall. He had cross-circuited the alarm system in her cabin.

"Gotcha!" he said, tears of laughter rolling down his cheeks.

Tash scowled. "Grow up!" she snapped angrily.

Zak chuckled, but the look on his sister's face took the fun out of his prank. "Hey, it was just a joke."

"Yeah, funny," she said coldly, "if you're in pre-school."

She turned and stalked down the hallway toward the cockpit, leaving her brother standing there with his crossed wires.

Tash trudged into the cockpit and slumped down in the copilot's seat. At first, Hoole ignored her as he busily punched commands into the ship's console. Finally, without looking her way, the Shi'ido said, "There was a disturbance back there. What was it?"

Tash gave her head a world-weary shake. "Zak, trying to play an immature joke." She sighed. "Kids."

Hoole glanced at her out of the corner of his dark eye. "Indeed."

Tash waited. When her uncle said nothing more, she added, "Why is he such a child? I mean, by the time I was his age I had already read half the library on Alderaan. Mom and Dad were talking about sending me to an academy for advanced students." Tash felt her throat tighten when she mentioned her parents. They had been killed when the Empire destroyed Alderaan, turning Zak and Tash into orphans with one blast of the Death Star's superlaser. "I mean," she went on, "why doesn't he just grow up?"

Hoole turned toward her, his long gray face unreadable. "He is growing up, Tash. In his own way."

"Well, he's sure taking his time about it," she said, looking down at her boots.

The Shi'ido cast a meaningful glance at her, but she missed it. "Perhaps he is in no hurry," Hoole said. "One should never be in a hurry to grow up."

He was about to say more, but a signal from the ship's hyperdrive indicated they were leaving hyperspace. They had arrived at Tatooine.

Hoole took the ship smoothly to sublight drive and steered it toward the giant yellow planet that appeared before them.

"Is it safe for us to visit Tatooine?" Tash asked as the ship entered the hot atmosphere. "We *are* wanted by the Empire, aren't we?"

"Yes," Hoole agreed. "But the Empire is a big place, and news doesn't always travel quickly. Besides, Tatooine is so remote, I doubt the Imperials here would even care about us."

The flight controllers at Mos Eisley gave them permission to land at Docking Bay Ninety-four, and Hoole guided the *Shroud* down to the landing platform. No one had asked them their business, and no Imperial ships had appeared to intercept them. Tash and Hoole met Zak in the corridor.

"You see," Hoole said to his niece, "there's absolutely no danger here."

He opened the hatch. But as he did, a white-armored

boot lashed out and kicked him in the stomach. The Shi'ido stumbled backward as five stormtroopers leaped into the ship, their blasters drawn.

One of the Imperials spoke from behind his armored helmet. "You are all under arrest."

CHAPTER

A fat Imperial officer waddled into the ship behind the troopers. His brown uniform barely held his belly in place. His chubby cheeks were damp and red from Tatooine's heat, but he managed to look threatening as he raised his blaster.

"Who are you?" the officer asked.

Tash held back a shudder. The Imperials had found them. She tensed, expecting to feel the deadly heat of a blaster bolt at any moment.

Hoole slowly rose to his feet. "I am an anthropologist," the Shi'ido explained without giving his name. "These are my . . . research assistants."

It was a bad lie, but the stormtrooper hardly noticed. "Where is Karkas?"

"Who?" Hoole asked.

"The criminal," Tash whispered.

The stormtrooper heard her. "Affirmative. He was spotted at the Koda Spaceport and then vanished. Three ships departed the spaceport at the time of his disappearance. Two of the ships, including this one, were tracked on courses for Tatooine. Now, where is he?"

Hoole carefully explained the mistake. They did not know Karkas, and they had certainly not allowed any criminals on board their ship. Tash told the officer that she had seen Karkas in the Koda cantina—and that the cantina's owner had told her about the mark Karkas left on his victims—but that they had not seen him since. Hoole concluded, "The fact that our ship left at the same time he disappeared is pure coincidence."

The Imperial official seemed to believe him—but only after his troopers had thoroughly searched the ship and found no sign of Karkas.

"Very well," the officer said. "You are free to go where you wish on Tatooine. But," he said, looking at Tash, "if you spot him again, inform me immediately. Contact the Imperial garrison here and ask for Commander Fuzzel." The officer tried to suck in his round gut as he said, "A good thing for you Karkas was not here. That fugitive has quite a price on his head. When I find him, I intend to make him regret the day he was born. Now, on your way."

Hoole, Zak, and Tash hurried out of the docking bay.

Zak cast a nervous glance back over his shoulder. "That

was not prime," he said as soon as the Imperials were out of earshot. "We could have ended up in a detention block faster than a Hutt can count credits."

"Indeed," Hoole said without turning around. "Fortunately for us, Commander Fuzzel was more concerned with finding Karkas than with checking our identification."

As they left the docking bay, they had to pass through another checkpoint. But this one was designed to track people leaving the planet. An Imperial soldier waved Hoole and the two Arrandas through as they examined the identification of two departing humans dressed in long brown robes.

"Those are the tallest Jawas I've ever seen," Zak said.

"They are not Jawas," Hoole said. "They are B'omarr monks. It is strange to see them out and about, let alone leaving the planet. The B'omarr monks usually keep to their chambers to study. Come, we must find transportation into the desert."

They tried to rent a landspeeder from a local merchant.

"Five hundred credits," the merchant demanded.

"What?" Zak and Tash gasped.

Hoole glanced back at the Imperial troopers patroling the town. "Very well," he said.

"But that's way too high," Tash insisted.

"Transports are in high demand," the dealer explained. "The Imperials say there is a lot of criminal activity on

Tatooine these days. They take speeders to use in their searches. Then the locals want speeders to avoid the Imperials. Bad news for you, but it keeps me in credits. By the way,'' the merchant added, ''what is your destination?''

Hoole paused. ''The palace of Jabba the Hutt.''

''In that case, the price is double,'' the merchant said, lowering his voice. ''I've lost too many speeders that way. Visitors go out to Jabba's palace . . . and they are never seen again.''

It took only three hours to ride from Mos Eisley to Jabba's palace, but the trek seemed much longer under the blaze of Tatooine's two suns. Just when Zak and Tash thought they would faint from the heat, Zak spied an enormous castle nestled among the rocks of a dry mountain range.

It was the palace of Jabba the Hutt, the most feared gangster in the galaxy.

Zak and Tash had been here before, but that didn't make them feel any safer. The fortress pulsed with danger. Jabba was as unpredictable as he was powerful. The fact that they had left Jabba's palace unharmed last time meant nothing. Many beings passed through his doors—never to be seen again.

They were admitted by the sentry droids, and then were stopped briefly by two Gamorrean guards—piglike creatures armed with huge axes. As they went on, a Twi'lek appeared out of the darkness. Two wormy tentacles grew out of the back of his head. The Twi'lek had draped the tentacles over his shoulders, and he stroked them thoughtfully as he studied the newcomers.

"Bib Fortuna," Hoole said, addressing the creature by its name. "I seek a meeting with Jabba."

"You return," Bib Fortuna whispered in a heavy accent. Tash noticed that his teeth were as sharp as fangs. "Perhaps Jabba not so generous with you this time, eh?"

"I'll take that chance," Hoole replied.

Fortuna let out a hiss from between his sharp teeth. Zak and Tash realized he was laughing. "Follow." Then he turned and walked down the corridor as silently as a wraith.

They hurried after Fortuna, who vanished through a round portal. Hoole, Zak, and Tash sped after him. Zak sprinted a little ahead of the others and was about to reach the portal when something scuttled out of the shadows.

Zak glanced over to see a giant spider ready to attack!

CHAPTER 4

"Help!" he shouted, leaping backward.

But the spider reversed course on spindly legs that made metallic clicks against the stone floor.

"Relax, Zak," Tash teased. "It's only a spider-shaped droid."

"Yeah," he replied. "But look what it's carrying."

Attached to the spider droid's small body was a glass jar filled with yellow-green liquid. Floating in the liquid was a solid mass of grooved gray matter. A brain.

"It's a brain spider," Tash said. "Remember? We saw one the last time we were here."

"Yeah, but what are they for?" Zak asked Hoole.

"We can discuss them later," Hoole replied. "We are at the throne room."

They stepped through the portal and looked down on a scene of utter chaos.

Jabba's audience chamber was just as Tash remembered it—crowded with aliens from a dozen worlds. There were gangsters, smugglers, thieves, and bounty hunters, all of whom lived in the shadows of the Empire. They hovered around Jabba's throne like dark moons orbiting a massive planet. Whenever anything illegal happened in the galaxy, Jabba the Hutt was sure to be at the center.

Something moved in the shadows nearby, and Zak jumped out of the way, thinking another brain spider had approached. Instead, something far more dangerous stepped into the light.

The bounty hunter Boba Fett.

Zak stared at the killer's helmet, which hid his face. Their paths had crossed once before, on a planet called Necropolis.

"Boba Fett!" Zak gasped. "I—I'm Zak Arranda. Remember me?"

The bounty hunter adjusted the blaster cradled in the crook of his arm.

Zak stammered, "Y-You saved me from being buried alive."

The man behind the mask said nothing. Zak saw his own reflection, twisted and warped, in the face of Boba Fett's helmet.

If Fett remembered him, he gave no sign. Without a word, the killer turned and stalked away.

Zak turned back to the center of the audience chamber. There, Jabba was talking to the local symbol of Imperial order and authority, Commander Fuzzel.

"He must have left for Jabba's palace right after we did," Tash whispered to Zak.

"Silence," Bib Fortuna warned.

In the audience chamber, Commander Fuzzel stood before Jabba's throne.

"Excellent work, Jabba," Commander Fuzzel was saying. "That's the third criminal you've turned in this month. The Empire thanks you."

From his platform, Jabba the Hutt rumbled a satisfied laugh. Tash noticed that the sluglike gangster looked bigger than the last time she'd seen him. He was growing fat on bowlfuls of live eels. "I'll take your thanks," the Hutt replied, "but I'd rather have the reward money. That criminal had a huge bounty on his head."

"You'll get the reward," Commander Fuzzel said. "All three criminals were wanted dead or alive, and I notice you turned them all in *dead*."

The Hutt grinned. "They're less trouble that way. I'll expect the credits to be in my account by morning. Goodbye, Commander."

Zak turned to Hoole and whispered, "What's a gangster like Jabba doing turning criminals over to the Empire?"

"Quiet," Hoole replied softly. "Listen."

"One more thing," Fuzzel said before leaving the audi-

27

ence chamber. "There's a rumor that the killer Karkas is on Tatooine. I want him. I'll pay double."

"Double?" Jabba mused. His voice sounded like a rumbling stomach. The alien crowd watching the conversation also murmured in surprise. "I will put my best people on it," Jabba replied. "Good day."

This time the Imperial official took the hint and turned around, carrying his rolls of fat out of Jabba's audience chamber. As he left, Hoole led Zak and Tash before the throne while Bib Fortuna whispered in the Hutt's ear.

"Well, well," Jabba growled. "What brings you three back to my doorstep?"

"Jabba," Hoole began. Jabba's seedy henchmen leaned forward to listen. So did Zak and Tash. Hoole hadn't told them what he planned to ask. The Shi'ido continued, "Years ago you did me a favor. When I was on the run from the Empire, you managed to erase my name and records from the Imperial networks so that I could continue to move around the galaxy without arousing suspicion." He paused. "I'd like to ask—as a *favor*—if you could do that again."

The crowd rumbled. Hoole had used the word *favor*. It was very dangerous to owe a Hutt a favor, because a Hutt always collected.

Jabba stared at Hoole, and a broad smile crossed his slimy face. The Hutt's thick pink tongue slithered out and ran along the edge of his lips.

"This can be done," he gurgled, "for a price. I have a job that requires someone with your particular talents."

Tash saw Hoole tense. This was the most dangerous part of the bargain. For years, she knew, Jabba had wanted to get Hoole on his payroll. The Shi'ido's shapechanging powers would make him an excellent spy, or even an assassin. She shook her head slowly. What if Jabba asked for something Hoole could not—or *would* not—do?

"Relax!" Jabba snorted. "I see the fear even in your stone face, Hoole!"

The crime lord waved toward Boba Fett, who had appeared near the Hutt's platform. "As you can see, I have all the assassins I need at the moment. No, this task is a little more . . . scholarly."

Jabba thumped his thick tail on the stone platform, and Bib Fortuna slithered forward. Carefully, he held up an ancient scroll. Both Tash and Zak gasped. They had grown up on computers, datadisks, and holographic projectors, just like their parents and grandparents before them. Paper books were rare treasures, and something as old as a scroll was almost unheard of.

"That has to be as old as the stars," Tash whispered.

Hoole looked down at the document without touching it. His eyes had barely skimmed the first few lines before they blazed with interest. "Do you know what this is?" he asked Jabba the Hutt.

Jabba shrugged his fat shoulders. "I know it's valuable

to the B'omarr monks. I found this scroll—along with a dozen others—in one of their tunnels. They've been begging to get it back ever since."

"*Are* you going to give it back?" the Shi'ido asked.

"Maybe," Jabba gurgled. "But first I want you to translate it. Translate this document for me, and I'll erase your names from the Empire's computer banks forever."

Tash had known Hoole long enough to read at least a few of his moods. Although his face was stern and motionless, she could tell by the way he leaned slightly forward, never taking his eyes off the scroll, that he wanted the job.

"Agreed," Hoole said, after waiting for almost a full minute.

"Excellent!" Jabba roared. "It will take a few days to break into the Imperial computer. That should give you time to do your research. Fortuna, show them to their rooms!" The Hutt thumped his fat tail on the stone platform, dismissing them.

As they left Jabba's throne room, Tash felt dread creep into her stomach, as though they had just made a deal with the dark side.

Fortuna showed them to their quarters. Hoole was given his own room, and Zak and Tash shared a small bedchamber next door. Without wasting a moment, Jabba's servant then escorted them through one of the many dark hallways in the palace. But unlike the others, this one led down into the cool darkness of Tatooine, far beneath the hot sand on the surface.

"Who are these B'omarr monks, anyway?" Zak whispered in the dark.

Tash clicked her tongue. "If you read more, you'd know they're the ones who built this place. This was their fortress, before Jabba came and took it away from them. Now Jabba lets them live only in the lowest levels of the palace."

"I wonder if we'll meet one," her brother said.

"Meet now," Bib Fortuna said, stopping suddenly. He seemed eager to get back to the action and intrigue of Jabba's throne room. "I go."

Fortuna vanished into the darkness just as another figure appeared. This one was smaller, and dressed in a brown robe and hood. He was about Zak's height, and when he pulled back his hood, they saw the face of a human boy. He looked about a year older than Tash. "Greetings," he said in a friendly voice. "Do you wish to visit the B'omarr monks?"

"Yes, we do," Hoole replied.

A grin spread across the boy's face. "Great!" he said in a very unmonklike fashion. Then he said more seriously, "I mean, you are welcome. We don't get many visitors here. My name is Brother Beidlo. But you can call me Beidlo. I will be your guide."

Beidlo led them down a long, curving hallway as he gave them a brief history of the B'omarr monks: how they had lived in the palace for years until Jabba arrived. Now the crime lord tolerated them as long as they didn't get in his way. Zak and Tash were fascinated by the things Beidlo said, but Hoole seemed more interested in studying lines of ancient writing that decorated the hallways.

Halfway down the corridor, Hoole stopped.

"These markings are quite similar to the writing on . . . the document I'm translating," he mused. "I must look at it again. Zak, Tash, let's go back."

"Oh," Beidlo said, disappointed. "But there's so much more to see."

"I wouldn't mind staying," Tash offered, trying to sound as mature as possible. "I mean, it's not often we get a chance for a guided tour. I'm sure it would be good experience."

Hoole considered. Tash and Zak could almost see his mind calculating how much trouble they might get into on their own. Finally, he agreed. "But keep an eye on a chrono. I want you back in our chambers by suppertime."

With their uncle gone, Zak and Tash picked up the pace of their steps and their questions. Zak couldn't help asking, "Don't the monks want their old homes back?"

Beidlo shrugged. "That's one of the things I don't understand yet. The monks don't seem to care. Every time I ask, they just tell me to push all such thoughts from my mind. I guess I'm just not enlightened enough."

"How long does it take to become enlightened?" Tash asked.

Beidlo shrugged. "It depends on the person. Some

monks advance very quickly, but for most of us, it takes years.''

"You seem like an awfully young monk," Tash observed.

Beidlo nodded. "I'm the newest member of the order."

"Is that why you get stuck with the job of greeting tourists?" Zak asked.

"That's right. The other monks are too busy with their studies," Beidlo said. "But I don't mind. It's nice to see new faces once in a while. This place gets pretty boring."

"Sounds like Tash's kind of place," Zak grunted. Then he added, "If you don't like it here, why stay?"

Beidlo shrugged. "I don't have anywhere else to go, really. My parents were killed by Sand People, and the B'omarr monks were willing to take me in. Besides, everything's not as dry as the desert around here. Come on, I'll show you."

Beidlo turned down another passageway. "You'll find this interesting. I'm going to show you the Great Room of the Enlightened."

"So, what do you monks do in the Great Room of the Enlightened, anyway?" Zak asked, half-joking. "Dark, mysterious things? Secret rituals?"

Beidlo chuckled. "Hardly. But we manage to keep busy," he said. "We meditate . . . and think . . . and consider . . . and concentrate. It's a full day!"

Zak and Tash followed Beidlo through a wide portal.

"Take it from someone who spends every day trying to become one," Beidlo added. "There's absolutely nothing dark, mysterious, or wicked about the B'omarr monks."

As he said this, he led his visitors into an enormous room. Shelves lined the walls, but Zak's and Tash's eyes were drawn to a crowd of brown-robed monks standing around a table.

As soon as the newcomers entered, the monks whirled around to face them. Angry eyes glared from beneath their hooded cloaks. One of the monks was holding something close to his body. Seeing what it was, Tash and Zak both gasped.

In his cupped hands, the monk held the squishy gray blob of a human brain.

CHAPTER 5

The monks came toward them. They glided so smoothly and soundlessly across the floor that they seemed to float like ghosts.

They began pushing Zak, Tash, and Beidlo out of the room. Old, wrinkled faces glared at them from beneath the tattered hoods. Beyond them, Tash caught sight of another monk lying on the table. She couldn't see clearly, but she thought the top of his skull had been removed.

The monk holding the brain quickly laid the gray blob in a clear plastic tray, then pointed one slime-covered hand at Beidlo and growled, ''Out.''

The monk didn't need to raise his voice. That one raspy word carried all the threat that was needed.

One of the monks activated a switch, and a heavy door rolled across the portal. Before it closed, Zak and Tash glimpsed the shelves on the walls. They were lined with jars, and inside each jar was a brain soaking in yellow-green soup.

"What's going on?" Zak demanded. "What are they doing to that man?"

Beidlo stood with his back to the wall. Even in the underground gloom they could see how pale his face had become. He groaned, "Oh, I'm in trouble! They'll never make me a monk now."

Tash grabbed Beidlo by the shoulders. "Beidlo, we've got to do something! They killed someone in there!"

Beidlo looked up as if suddenly realizing Zak and Tash were still there. "Him? Oh, no, no!" he said quickly. "You don't understand. They're not killing him. They're giving him eternal life."

"Right," Zak scoffed. "If that's true, then a coffin's just a permanent home."

Beidlo seemed more amused than alarmed. He sighed. "Listen, those monks are pretty old-fashioned. They got angry because I accidentally let outsiders into one of the brain transference ceremonies. But there's another monk I want you to meet. He'll explain everything."

Beidlo started down the hallway.

Zak and Tash looked at each other.

"What should we do?" Tash wondered aloud.

Zak scowled at her. "Don't ask me. You're the one who's all grown up, remember?"

"How could I forget?" Tash retorted. "I've got you here to remind me what a child acts like."

She started down the hall after Beidlo, leaving Zak to shake his head. If this was growing up, he wanted no part of it.

"Teenagers," he sighed, and hurried to catch up.

Zak and Tash followed Beidlo to a wide chamber filled with stone benches and tables. The room was large enough to hold a hundred monks, but the place was empty except for a solitary figure sitting in the corner.

"This is the monks' tea room," Beidlo explained. "Most of the B'omarr who aren't at the brain transference ceremony are off meditating right now, but I knew Grimpen would be here."

Before Tash and Zak could respond, the lone monk rose to his feet, threw back his hood, and greeted them with a warm smile. His hair was gray, but his face looked young, and his eyes were bright and clear blue.

"Welcome, welcome!" the monk said with a hearty laugh. "It's not often we get strangers in our halls. My name is Brother Grimpen. You can skip the *Brother* part if you like."

Tash laughed. "Thanks. One brother's enough for me, anyway."

Zak frowned at her.

Tash ignored him and continued, "You're much friendlier than the other monks we just met."

37

Grimpen nodded sympathetically. "Many of our monks have lost their sense of politeness. Please forgive them."

"Politeness!" Zak said. "I thought those monks would kill us when we went into that Great Room of Enlightenment!"

Beidlo cast an embarrassed look at the older monk. "It was my fault. I accidentally interrupted a brain transference ceremony."

"Oh, that," Grimpen said with a wave of his hand. "Some of the old-timers think everything has to be such a secret. It makes them grumpy. They don't want outsiders getting hold of the B'omarr knowledge."

"You don't feel the same way?" Tash asked.

Grimpen looked into her eyes. She felt like she would fall into the deep blue of his gaze as he said, "I think knowledge should be for everyone. Wisdom may be found in many places. You, for instance. I sense that you are wise beyond your years."

Zak groaned inwardly. Why was this monk trying so hard to compliment Tash?

Aloud, Zak said, "What's all this about brain transference, anyway?"

Grimpen explained: "It's part of the B'omarr tradition. We seal ourselves off from distractions so we can concentrate more on the mysteries of the universe. Over the years, we become more and more enlightened. When we reach a certain stage of enlightenment, our brains are transferred out of our bodies into glass jars.''

"So we saw," Zak said. "And I guess sometimes those glass jars are attached to spider droids?"

"Correct," Grimpen said. "This allows the enlightened ones to move around and experience different surroundings while remaining detached from the world. That way, the enlightened can continue to think without distractions like hunger or sleep."

"The brain spiders take care of that for them?" Zak asked, impressed.

Grimpen nodded. "The droids keep the brains alive and healthy. Since you and I have bodies, we worry about eating, and sleeping, and getting tired. We get cold and hot. Inside the brain jars, the enlightened monks don't have to worry about any of that."

"Can they talk?" Zak asked, curious about the technology.

Grimpen shook his head. "It's possible to give them electronic voices," he said, "but Jabba the Hutt controls the palace. He grew tired of hearing the enlightened ones try to teach him their lessons, and he ordered all the voice boxes removed. Now, all the enlightened ones can do is think about the ultimate truth of the galaxy."

The ultimate truth of the galaxy? Tash was amazed. *Sounds like they're looking for the Force.* "What *is* this ultimate truth?" she asked Grimpen.

Grimpen smiled knowingly. "Somehow, I think you know already."

Tash blushed. "Spending all your time thinking and studying sounds like my idea of a perfect life."

"Yeah, perfectly boring," Zak muttered. "Look, Tash, it's time to get going."

Grimpen put a gentle hand on Tash's shoulder and held her eyes with his. "Tash, I sense that you have the potential for great enlightenment. You are welcome to visit and study here whenever you wish. There is much we can teach someone as wise as you."

"What a load of bantha fodder," Zak grumbled as he and Tash returned to the upper levels of Jabba's palace.

"You're just jealous because he didn't pay any attention to you," Tash replied.

"Jealous?" Zak repeated in disbelief. "Jealous because I was ignored by a guy whose goal in life is to have his brain stuck in a jar? You've gone hyper."

Tash shrugged. Deep down, she knew Zak had a point—the B'omarr monks did have some strange practices. But they were also devoted to knowledge and learning, and that appealed to her. She had always loved reading and studying.

Besides, she thought, she had already begun to feel the Force. She had even used it once or twice. Maybe studying with Grimpen would help her develop her powers.

Tash and Zak reached their quarters to find Hoole standing at a round viewport in his room, staring out onto the hot desert sand. He hardly noticed when his niece and nephew entered the room.

"Uncle Hoole?" Zak asked. "Is something wrong?"

Hoole said quietly, "I met with Jabba the Hutt again while you were down below. Apparently, he can't erase our records from the Imperial computers."

"Why not?" Zak asked. "Didn't he do it for you once before?"

Hoole nodded. "Yes, but that was years ago. Apparently, with so much Rebel activity, the Empire has tightened security. Ever since the Rebellion stole the Death Star plans and destroyed the space station, it's become impossible to splice into Imperial databanks."

"Then there's nothing he can do," Tash concluded.

Hoole let out a small sigh, hardly more than a breath. "He offered to supply us with new names, new identities. He said no one would know they were fakes. We could become completely new people."

"New identities?" Tash said, her eyes brightening. "That sounds great. We can be anyone we want to be!"

"Prime!" Zak agreed. "It'll be like we're spies."

Hoole's frown deepened. After a pause, he said, "We would not be spies. Spies pretend to be other people for a short time. We would actually have to abandon our old selves. Leave our names behind forever. Become totally new individuals."

"I could live with that," Tash said.

"I could not," Hoole said. "I may reject Jabba's offer."

"What!" Tash and Zak cried together. "Why?" Tash added. "It sounds like the perfect solution."

Hoole glowered. "You would not understand." He refused to say anything more.

The evening and night passed slowly in their quarters. Hoole remained deep in thought. Tash dug a datapad out of her pack and read everything she could find on the B'omarr monks.

Zak sat on his bed, wishing the others weren't so determined to be serious.

The next day, Hoole rose early to continue his work on the B'omarr scrolls. "Until I make my final decision," he explained, "I will continue to work on those scrolls. Besides, they are worth studying." He paused meaningfully. "I want you both to understand that this is not a vacation. Jabba has extended his hospitality to us, but this is still a dangerous place. Be careful."

The minute he was gone, Tash started toward the tunnels of the B'omarr monks.

"Hey!" Zak said. "Uncle Hoole just finished telling us to stay out of trouble."

"I'm not getting into trouble," Tash responded. "Besides, he also said it was important to study the B'omarr monks."

"Important for *him*, not for *you*," her brother retorted.

But Tash was already gone.

Zak caught up with her just as she reached the monks' tea room again. Surprisingly, it wasn't hard to find. The

B'omarr monks were very orderly, and their tunnels were laid out in neat, organized rows.

They found Beidlo in the tea room, using an old-fashioned push broom to sweep sand off the floor. His face lit up when he saw Zak and Tash. "I'm glad you're back! I'll be done with my chores in half an hour; then I can show you more of the tunnels. There are some excellent caverns, and even a few—"

"Actually," Tash confessed, "I was just looking for Brother Grimpen."

"Oh," Beidlo said. He looked disappointed. "All right. He's down that way." The young monk pointed toward a hallway at the end of the room.

"Thanks," Tash said, moving on.

"Don't feel bad," Zak said to Beidlo. "She's been doing that to me for a couple of days now. I'll talk to you later." He hurried after his sister.

"Tash!" Grimpen called out as they moved down the dark tunnel. The monk seemed to step out of the darkness itself. "So good to see you again," Grimpen said to Tash, barely nodding at Zak.

"I had some free time," Tash explained, "and you said we were welcome—"

"Of course, of course!" Grimpen said approvingly. "In fact, your timing is perfect. I was just going back to my private rooms to meditate. If you're really interested in the B'omarr ways, it's a perfect chance to learn."

"Let's go," Tash said.

"Um, Tash," Zak said, grabbing hold of her sleeve. "I'm not sure that's such a good idea. What would Uncle Hoole say about us going off with some stranger?"

Tash's eyes were like lasers blasting her younger brother. "You're starting to sound like a baby-sitter, and I don't need a baby-sitter, Zak. Besides, Grimpen is a monk. It's not like he's one of Jabba's henchmen."

"Exactly right," Grimpen said.

Zak gave up with a sigh. The strange thing was the more Tash wanted to be a grown-up, the more she behaved like a child. And the more Zak wanted her to be her old, thirteen-year-old self, the more *he* sounded like an adult.

Why couldn't things just stay the way they were? he thought as he hurried to catch up. Beyond the tea room, the tunnels became more confusing. Zak found more twists and turns, and he nearly lost sight of Tash and Grimpen twice as they made sharp turns down smaller side tunnels, winding their way deeper into the catacombs of the ancient B'omarr temple.

". . . There are many stages of spiritual growth," Grimpen was explaining to Tash. "At each stage, there is a test to make sure the monk understands what he has learned."

Tash, Zak, and Grimpen passed a pair of monks walking in the opposite direction. Beneath their hoods, the monks scowled at the two Arrandas. Zak had the strange sensation that the angry old monks wanted to see *his* brain on a shelf. He swallowed.

44

"What are the tests like?" Tash asked.

"Sometimes the tests are very easy, like answering questions or reciting passages from the ancient writings," Grimpen said. Up ahead, Zak and Tash caught sight of a faint light source. "And sometimes the tests are physical, to test how well a monk uses his mind over matter."

Grimpen stopped. Before them lay the source of the light they'd seen a moment before. They stood at the edge of a glowing bed of hot coals. Steam rose from the thick layer of fiery rocks, and now and then a rock would crack into smaller burning embers with a loud *pop!* The bed of coals stretched from wall to wall across the tunnel, and was far too wide to jump across.

"What's this?" Tash asked.

Grimpen flashed her a confident smile. "This is your first test, Tash."

Tash blinked. "But how—?"

"Like this," Grimpen replied. Then, calmly, he stepped onto the blazing coals. Zak winced, but Grimpen looked as if he were calmly walking across a field of grass. Step by step, he crossed the coal bed as light and flames licked at his ankles, and steam rose up around his face.

He reached the other side unharmed.

Grimpen stretched out his hand to Tash. "Your turn."

Zak grabbed Tash's arm. "You're beyond hyper if you do that."

Tash shook her arm free of Zak's hold. "If he did it, I can do it."

Grimpen nodded. "All you have to do is believe, Tash. This is your pathway to a whole new life, a whole new way of seeing the galaxy."

Tash paused, but only for a moment. Grimpen was offering her what she wanted—something that Uncle Hoole and even Zak could not give her.

"Don't do it, Tash," Zak warned.

"Relax," she replied.

She stepped onto the burning coals. As she did, she vanished into a cloud of steam.

And screamed.

CHAPTER

6

"Tash!" Zak cried. He leaped to the edge of the burning coals, reaching through the steam.

But Tash's scream hadn't been a cry for help.

"It doesn't hurt!" she shouted in excitement. "It's not hot at all!"

"Of course not," Grimpen called back. "Once your mind reaches a certain advanced stage, normal sensations like heat and cold no longer mean anything. It's mind over matter."

The steam cleared momentarily, and Zak saw his sister step across to the other side of the coal bed. Zak couldn't believe it. He looked down at the coals and saw Tash's footprints clearly in the glowing rock. Wherever her steps had crushed a rock, tiny flames shot up, leaving a fiery trail.

"What about me?" Zak called out to Tash.

"You are welcome to join us," Grimpen said. "If you have the strength of mind, all you have to do is cross."

Zak studied the coals again. He was tempted to try. But Tash had the Force on her side—he had seen her use it in the past.

"No thanks," he replied.

Grimpen shrugged. "Then we will say good-bye. Come on, Tash, there are many things I can teach you." Tash glanced back at her brother for a moment, then turned and disappeared.

Zak stood alone in the tunnel. "Oh, frag," he whispered. "It's not fair."

He was somewhere in Jabba's palace—he didn't know where. He'd been walking for an hour, turning down whatever passageway caught his eye, going through whichever doors were open. Sometimes short-snouted Gamorrean guards appeared and pushed him away, not allowing him through certain portals, but Zak didn't care. He just turned and walked in another direction.

Zak had lost friends before. He'd even lost members of his family. Everyone he had ever known was wiped out when the Empire destroyed Alderaan. But this was different. Tash wasn't the victim of some Imperial plot. She wasn't being forced to leave. She had *chosen* to leave him behind.

He hadn't felt so abandoned since the day his parents died.

Click-click-click. Click-click-click.

"Maybe it's me," he wondered aloud.

His voice echoed down the hallway, making him feel even lonelier.

Click-click-click.

Under the echoes of his voice, Zak heard something scratching on the stone floor, but he was too deep in thought to pay much attention.

Tash is older than me. Maybe she is just growing up. Maybe I am too much of a kid for her now, and I'm just in her way.

Click-click-click-click-click.

He frowned. Leaving a friend behind didn't seem like a very grown-up thing to do. It wasn't something his mom and dad would have done. It wasn't even something Uncle Hoole would do.

Click-click-click-click-click-click!

Suddenly, Zak realized that the noise had become louder. It sounded like a dozen metal knives being dropped to the ground, one after another. "What—?" Zak started to ask.

A brain spider shuffled out of the darkness.

"Oh, great," Zak muttered.

The mechanical spider took a few more steps. *Click-click-click!* Then it stopped a meter away from Zak. In the center of its metal body, he could see the gray brain floating in a greenish liquid in its transparent container. The spider's servos hummed as if it were waiting.

"What, am I in *your* way, too?" Zak said sarcastically. He stepped to the left to clear a path for the spider.

The spider followed him.

"All right, I'll go the other way." Zak stepped to the right.

So did the brain spider.

"What do you want?" he asked it.

But the brain spider couldn't answer.

Zak frowned. "I'm in no mood to dance with droids, thanks, so I'll be going." He took one step back, and then another.

The brain spider followed.

As Zak took a few more steps, the creeping brain-carrier matched his movements. When he sped up, the brain spider increased its speed. It had no eyes, but Zak was overcome by the sensation that the brain itself was . . . *staring* at him.

"This is not prime," he whispered, and turned to run.

The brain spider ran after him.

Clickclickclickclickclickclickclickclickclick!

"Help!" Zak called out. "Help me!"

"Help . . . help . . . me . . . ," his echo called back to him.

Where was he? How far had he come?

Zak didn't know the answer. But by the sound of its clicking legs, the brain spider was closing in on him. He didn't want to find out what those metal limbs would do if they caught him.

A small glowpanel set in the wall ahead revealed a narrow opening and a steep staircase. Without slowing, Zak plunged through the doorway and scampered down the stairs.

Behind him, he could hear the brain spider slow, then stop. It wasn't following him anymore!

Lit only by a faint glowpanel every dozen meters or so, the stairs spun their way for two hundred steps down into the planet. At the bottom, Zak paused to catch his breath. There was still no sound from the brain spider.

He saw a set of gates that led into a wide corridor. The gates were made of thick durasteel bars.

"A dungeon?" he muttered.

Two voices echoed from down the corridor, breaking the silence. He crept forward. If he wasn't supposed to be here, he didn't want to get caught—even if he could explain why he'd run down the stairs.

A dozen meters farther on, the corridor met another hallway, with paths leading left and right. The voices were coming from the left. They were whispering, but Zak was able to catch some of the words.

"I can't stand this waitin'," rasped one angry voice. "I'm not used to waitin' for anything."

A deeper voice rumbled back, "Be patient. You'll have your chance soon enough." Zak was sure the second speaker was Jabba the Hutt.

Creeping forward, Zak peeked around the corner. The hallway wasn't well lit, but he clearly saw the bulky figure of the crime lord. Next to him stood a huge human. By the dim light on his face, Zak saw that one of the human's eyes had been nearly crushed.

"How soon?" crush-face growled. "This planet's been crawlin' with Imperials ever since those Rebels blasted outta here ten months ago. I didn't come all this way just to get thrown into a detention center."

The Hutt said, "You'll have no fear of Imperials. Just wait one more day, Karkas."

Karkas? Zak thought. Hadn't the Imperials been looking for someone named Karkas? What was he doing here, and why was Jabba helping him, and not turning him in for the reward?

Click-click-click.

Zak heard the sound trickle down the staircase behind him. The brain spider had followed him down the stairs. If Jabba and his companion heard the noise, they ignored it.

"One more day," Karkas agreed.

Click-click. Zak looked around for another way out. There was none.

"Until then," Jabba said. Zak heard the wet, squishy sound of the Hutt slithering along the stone floor.

Just in time, Zak thought. He dashed forward. The voices had come from the left, so he cut to the right and ran as quickly and quietly as he could.

Speeding through the gloomy tunnels, Zak finally found an open door. He leaped through the door, hoping to find another tunnel that would lead him back to the higher levels. Instead, he saw only three thick walls.

He had reached a dead end.

Zak spun around just in time to see a heavy door slide shut behind him. A small set of polished bars guarded a tiny window in the door.

Zak had walked into one of Jabba's prison cells.

And now he was locked inside.

CHAPTER

"Hey!" Zak yelled. "Let me out! Somebody let me out!"

Click-click-click.

Zak watched through the bars as the brain spider approached. It shuffled up to the cell door and straightened its legs, raising the brain up to its full height. The brain seemed to be studying Zak through its transparent jar.

Zak shuddered. "Well, at least you can't get me," he whispered. "So why don't you get back to your study or your meditation or whatever it is you do."

The spider turned and shuffled away.

Once the spider was gone, Zak filled his lungs with air and shouted as loudly as he could. "Help! Someone help! I'm stuck in here!"

He yelled until his voice went hoarse. Then he paused to listen. A voice answered.

"That won't do any good."

It came from across the hall. The light was dim, but Zak could just make out another cell across the way, and a prisoner inside with his face pressed against the barred window.

"But I got in here by accident," Zak explained.

"I know," said the prisoner. "I saw you. But that won't matter. No one comes down here but the Gamorreans, and they don't speak Basic."

"You mean I'm stuck here?"

The prisoner nodded. "But it won't be for long. From what I hear, none of the prisoners stay for long."

"You mean they go free?" Zak asked.

"I didn't say that," the man replied.

Zak swallowed. "But when they see me, they'll know there's been a mistake. They'll know I didn't do anything."

A grim laugh came from the other cell. "Neither did I. I just came here thinking of joining the B'omarr monks. I thought they'd accept me, too. I even passed some of their tests. One of them said I had great potential. The next thing I knew, Jabba's goons had thrown me in prison."

The B'omarr monks. Zak was beginning to get a bad feeling about them. Why were they so secretive? Why had one of their brain spiders chased him? And why had they let this man get thrown into Jabba's dungeon? Zak heaved a frustrated sigh. If Tash had been with him, he knew they'd have figured it out together.

As his eyes adjusted to the deep gloom of his cell, Zak

looked around his tiny prison. There were no chairs, not even a cot. A skeleton lay on the floor next to the door. One arm had been stretched forward, scratching at the door. The bones were dry and brittle. Whoever the prisoner had been, he had died long ago. By the looks of his untouched bones, the guards seemed to have simply forgotten about him.

Looking closer, Zak realized that the prisoner hadn't been scratching at the door, he'd been chipping at the stones with a small knife. The blade was rusted and old now, but it still looked solid. Trying not to touch the old bones, Zak took the knife from the skeleton's hand.

Examining the chipped stone where the prisoner had been working, Zak saw the outline of an access panel.

"It must control the door mechanism," he said.

The poor dead captive had nearly chipped his way into the panel, but he must have grown too weak. Getting a good grip on the knife, Zak went to work.

"Hope you don't mind if I finish the job," he said to the skeleton. "It's just that I don't want to end up like you."

Zak had nearly broken through to the wiring that controlled his cell door.

"Hey, what are you doing?" called the voice from across the hall.

"Trying to get out of here," Zak replied between blows with the rusty knife. "Almost got it."

"Hey!" said the other prisoner. "If you get out, will you free me, too?"

Zak paused. He knew about Jabba the Hutt's reputation for cruelty. For all he knew, the other prisoner might be as innocent as he was. On the other hand, he might be a *real* criminal. Zak remembered that Jabba had already turned three wanted criminals in to the Imperials. Maybe this was yet another killer.

"I don't know," he said at last. "How do I know you're not in here for a good reason?"

"I didn't do anything!" the man yelled. "You gotta believe me!"

Clunk!

One last stroke of the knife opened a small hole in the wall, exposing a tangle of wires. Zak didn't know which one powered the automatic door, so he just cut them all with a quick slash of the knife. There was a groan of metal rollers, and the locks that held the prison door in place suddenly relaxed. Zak grabbed hold of the bars and pulled. The door was heavy, but he managed to open it enough to squeeze through.

"You did it!" the other prisoner cheered. "Now, please, let me out!"

Zak stepped closer to the other cell door. The prisoner was human, with a large nose and long hair. His features were smooth. He looked more like a scholar than a criminal.

Zak hesitated. Suppose he made a mistake and freed a wanted criminal? Wouldn't that make him an accomplice?

But if the man really was innocent, and Zak abandoned

him, he'd be helping Jabba the Hutt with one of his many crimes.

Zak wavered, unsure of what to do. Either way, he might make a terrible mistake.

"If you're innocent," he said, "why did Jabba throw you in jail?"

"I told you I don't know!" the man said. "Please help me!"

Zak decided. The man just didn't seem like a criminal to him. Locating the door controls, Zak unlocked the cell. The door slid open, and the man stepped forward. He was very slender, with smooth hands. He cried out in relief as he slipped through the door.

"Thanks! That's one I owe you!" the man said. "Now I'm getting out of here as fast as I can!" He bolted away into the darkness.

Zak was about to follow, but five pointy fingernails dug into his shoulder and a voice snarled in his ear, "What are you doing here?"

CHAPTER 8

Zak spun around and found himself face-to-face with the pale, oily visage of Bib Fortuna. Fortuna's sharp teeth bit into his lower lip as he glared at Zak.

"I got lost," Zak explained. "I accidentally stumbled into one of the prison cells and it took me a while to get out."

Fortuna spied the two open doors. "Where is the other prisoner?" he demanded.

"Prisoner?" Zak said. "What prisoner?"

Another growl escaped from between the alien's teeth. "Never mind. This place is restricted. Do not come here again or you will become a permanent resident."

Zak didn't argue. Fortuna showed him the way out, and Zak hurried back to the upper levels. He rushed into

Hoole's quarters, where he found the Shi'ido poring over the B'omarr manuscripts.

"Very interesting," Hoole said, more to himself than to Zak. "These B'omarr monks have developed some fascinating practices." He pointed to some of the markings on the scroll. To Zak, they looked like a bunch of scribbles.

"See here," Hoole explained. "Sometimes the B'omarr used tricks to convince their students that they had mind control power. One of the tricks involved lume rocks."

"Lume rocks, right," Zak said, still catching his breath. "But Uncle Hoole—"

"They're quite clever," Hoole continued. "They appear to give off light and heat, but they don't actually burn the skin. The B'omarr monks tell the students to hold them, and the students think they're using their minds to resist the heat."

That got Zak's attention. He recalled the test Grimpen had given Tash. " 'Hot coals,' my afterburners," he grumbled.

"What was that?" Hoole asked.

More loudly, Zak asked, "You mean these monks are actually fakes?"

"Not exactly," Hoole explained. "These tricks are used to build confidence in the students. The monks believe that if the students *think* they can do certain things long enough, eventually they can. In addition, the monks are the only beings that have achieved the ability to do brain transference, and—"

"Uncle Hoole, listen," Zak interrupted. "Something really strange is going on. First I was chased into the dungeons by a brain spider. And I met someone there who I'm sure was innocent so I freed him and—"

"Wait a moment," Hoole demanded. He gave Zak a look that made the young Arranda's heart skip a beat. "You went into Jabba's dungeon? You *freed* a prisoner? That was extremely unwise."

"There's more," Zak continued. "I overhead Jabba the Hutt talking to someone named Karkas. That's the criminal the Imperials are after! It sounded like they were working together."

Hoole nodded. "Very well, Zak. Thank you for the information. Now, please, do not wander away from our rooms again." He turned back to his scrolls.

Zak's jaw dropped. "Uncle Hoole! Aren't you going to do anything?"

Hoole looked up. "What should I do?"

Zak was dumbstruck. Was this really his uncle? Hoole was usually the first to act when he saw something bad happening. "I don't know," Zak replied, "call the Imperials, confront Jabba. Karkas is wanted in two dozen star systems!"

Hoole sighed. "Zak, Jabba is a gangster. I am sure that you are right—Jabba is up to something. But there is no way I can stop it. Not while we are under his roof. I do not agree with his methods, but considering Jabba's power, there is very little we can do about it at the moment. You are being a little naive.''

''Naive?'' Zak tried to get his mouth around the new word.

''It means young and innocent,'' Hoole explained.

''*Young* again,'' Zak groaned. ''You're starting to sound like Tash.''

''Speaking of whom,'' the Shi'ido said, ''where is your sister? You two are usually inseparable.''

Zak grimaced. ''She made friends with one of the B'omarr monks. I guess she'd rather be with him than with me.'' Zak was hoping his uncle would hear the frustration in his voice, but Hoole was too preoccupied.

''Considering what you have just told me, I think it might be best if you and Tash stay here for a while. Please go down to the B'omarr tunnels and find her. And Zak—'' he said with a knowing look, ''stay out of Jabba the Hutt's business.''

Zak grumbled to himself as he left Hoole's room. First his sister abandoned him, then his uncle called him naive, and now he'd become an errand boy.

Zak walked down the hall nervously. At any moment he expected someone to jump out at him. But nothing happened. He passed two or three beings who either ignored him or nodded in his direction. Bib Fortuna drifted across his path, hardly noticing the young human.

Everything was as normal as it could be in the palace of Jabba the Hutt.

Uncle Hoole's right, Zak thought as he descended into the B'omarr tunnels. *I have to remember where I am. Wanted criminals and innocent prisoners aren't out of the ordinary here. There's nothing for* me *to worry about.*

The tunnels were deserted. Keeping an eye out for brain spiders, Zak tried to remember where the monks' tea room was, figuring he'd find someone there who could help him locate Tash.

"Psst! Zak!" a voice whispered.

Zak looked around. No one was there.

"Over here!" The voice came from a dark corner where the corridor curved. Stepping into the corner, Zak saw Brother Beidlo huddled there. He looked frightened.

"What is it?" Zak asked.

"Keep your voice down," Beidlo warned.

Two monks appeared in the hallway, and Beidlo pulled Zak into the darkness. The young monk pressed his back against the wall until the B'omarr had passed.

"You have to get out of here," Beidlo told Zak in a frightened whisper. "We all do. Or we're all going to end up dead!"

CHAPTER

The look of fear on Beidlo's face was so intense that Zak thought he might be crazy. "What do you mean?" he asked. "This morning you said everything was just fine."

"That was before"—Beidlo swallowed—". . . before I found out about the brain transfers."

Zak scratched his head. His mind was cluttered enough without Beidlo confusing him further. "But you told us about the brain transfers. You just about showed us one!"

"I know! I know!" Beidlo explained. "That's how it started. There wasn't supposed to be a brain transfer yesterday. It made me curious, so I started looking around. I found out that there have been an awful lot of unscheduled brain transfers recently. Then I realized there are at least twice as many brain spiders as there were when I joined the B'omarr just a few months ago."

"So?" Zak asked. "Doesn't that just mean more monks are becoming enlightened or whatever?"

"Either that," Beidlo said in a trembling voice, "or someone is removing their brains against their will."

"What?" Zak said in disbelief. "That doesn't make any sense. Why would someone want to stick their brains in little jars? Besides, Uncle Hoole just told me that only the B'omarr monks know how to perform the operation. Which means they're doing it to themselves."

Beidlo shook his head. "No, no, it's worse than that. Ten monks have supposedly become enlightened in the past few months. But there have been fifteen operations! And I'm telling you, there are way too many brain spiders around. And they're acting strangely."

Zak remembered the brain spider that had chased him. "I can't argue with that."

"Something bad is happening here," Beidlo nearly sobbed. "Someone is performing the brain transfers on monks who aren't ready!"

Zak swallowed. "Okay, if this is true, why tell me? Why not tell the other monks?"

Beidlo smacked his head in frustration. "Don't you think I tried that? But the monks just don't care. I told you, they spend all their time studying and thinking. They don't care what happens to their bodies. They don't care about anything outside their meditation. They won't listen!"

"And you think I will," Zak guessed.

65

"You and your uncle. Please, call the authorities. Ask them to come down here and investigate. Anything!"

Zak wasn't sure what to think. He didn't know anything about brain spiders or B'omarr monks. Beidlo's story didn't make very much sense. But he still had the nagging feeling that something weird was going on in Jabba's palace. "Okay, I'll tell my uncle. Maybe he'll have an idea."

"Thank you!" Beidlo said in relief. "While you do that, I'm going to tell the one monk who might be willing to act. Grimpen's not like the rest. He'll get to the bottom of this!"

Zak hurried up the tunnel as Beidlo ran in the opposite direction. Armed with this new information, Zak returned to his uncle's quarters.

"Back so soon?" Hoole asked. "Where's Tash?"

Zak quickly explained what Beidlo had told him.

Hoole frowned. "I do not understand, Zak. What would the monks have to gain by doing more brain transfers? And why would they do them on anyone but other monks?"

"I don't know," Zak replied, "but I'm telling you, something's wrong here."

The Shi'ido nodded. "I think you're right, Zak. Come on."

Hoole returned to the B'omarr tunnels with Zak, and together they searched for Tash. They searched in the hallways, they searched in the tea room, they even found a small library—but there was no sign of Tash.

Once in a while, a brown-robed monk would wander by.

66

Hoole would stop the monk and ask if he had seen a young human girl. But each time, the monk merely stared at Hoole for a moment, then walked on without saying a word.

"Friendly bunch," Zak sighed.

"Let's continue," Hoole said.

They looked for nearly an hour, but there was no sign of Tash. Finally, just as they were about to give up, another monk approached. Zak decided to try once more.

"Excuse me," he said, "but have you seen— Oh, Beidlo, it's you!"

Beidlo blinked as though he'd been daydreaming. "Huh? Oh, yes, it's me. What can I do for you?"

"What can y-you . . . ?" Zak stammered. "I warned Uncle Hoole, just like you wanted. Now we're looking for Tash."

Beidlo looked confused and seemed annoyed. "What are you talking about?"

"You know what I'm talking about," Zak exclaimed. "The brain transfers! An hour ago, you were terrified that everyone was going to die."

"Oh, yes, that. Don't worry about it. I think I was wrong."

"Excuse me, young man," Hoole interjected. "Are you saying that there is nothing out of the ordinary going on here?"

"Yes, that's what I'm saying," Beidlo said. "Now excuse me, I've got . . . things to do."

Beidlo pushed past them and hurried along the tunnel.

Hoole cast a scolding glance at Zak.

"Uncle Hoole, I—"

"I don't blame you, Zak," Hoole interrupted. "Jabba's palace can be quite confusing. But you must understand, this isn't like any other place you've been. Strangeness and danger are normal here."

Zak didn't argue . . . but he didn't agree, either. Beidlo had been terrified only a short time ago. Now he hardly seemed to remember the conversation.

"I'm not suggesting you did anything wrong, Zak," Hoole said as they returned to their chambers. "It is simply that this place is too full of intrigue for someone your age. That's not your fault—it is just a question of experience. You will be much safer if you stay near me."

Hoole reached his own room and pointed to Zak's quarters next door.

"I promise you," he said, "that as long as you stay near your room, nothing bad will happen."

"Yes, Uncle Hoole," Zak said sullenly. He walked into his room.

And found Tash hanging upside down from the ceiling like a piece of meat on a hook.

CHAPTER

10

"Tash!" he yelled at the top of his lungs.

"What!" she screamed back. Her eyes flew open and she plummeted headlong toward the floor, where she landed with a heavy thud. Zak saw a small bar attached to a rope dangling from the ceiling. Tash had been hanging from the bar by her feet.

"Thanks a lot, laser brain!" Tash said, sitting up and rubbing her head. "You nearly scared the life out of me."

"I scared *you*?" Zak retorted. "What in space were you doing hanging from the ceiling?"

Tash sighed like a weary teacher explaining a lesson to a thick headed student. "It's a B'omarr meditation exercise. Grimpen showed me how to do it."

"I knew that monk had you turned inside out, but I

didn't know he had you turned upside down as well," Zak said snidely.

"Funny," his sister replied. "Just the kind of thing I'd expect from someone as unenlightened as you."

Zak smirked. "Oh, like you're so wise."

Tash got to her feet and limped around for a moment to make sure her leg wasn't damaged. "According to Grimpen, I am. He says only one person in a billion has the potential that I have."

"Great," Zak said under his breath, "you're still taking compliments from a guy who wants to have his brain removed."

More loudly, he said, "Listen, Tash, I know we haven't been getting along too well, but I need your help. There's something odd going on. First I was chased by a brain spider. Then I met this prisoner, and now Beidlo is acting very strange—"

"Zak." Tash held up one hand to stop him. "I'm sorry if I've been rude to you. I don't mean to be. It's just that meeting Grimpen has opened my eyes. You know how much I like to study, and you know that I'm trying to figure out how to use the Force. The B'omarr meditations Grimpen has shown me really help. I feel like I'm starting to understand things."

"Great. So try to understand this," Zak continued. He told her about Beidlo's strange behavior.

Tash shrugged. Her face took on a distant look. "It

70

sounds as if everything worked itself out, Zak. I have more important things to think about."

"More important!" Zak sputtered. "What's more important than making sure we're all safe? I suppose now you're going to hang from the ceiling by your big toe?"

Tash's face turned red, but she made a great effort to remain calm. She forced her face to look relaxed and walked out of the room.

"You handled that very well," said Grimpen. She had returned to his chamber.

"Thanks," Tash said. She liked listening to his voice. Grimpen seemed to know her very well. He always found the good in her. "But I can't stay here long. Uncle Hoole told us not to go too far from our quarters."

"I understand," Grimpen said sympathetically. He was sitting cross-legged in his small meditation room. "But I'm glad you told me about Zak. Tash, this may be hard to hear, but I think you're wise enough to understand. Sometimes, as we become more enlightened, our friends become jealous. They try to hold us back." He looked deeply into her eyes. "I think Zak is holding you back."

Tash nodded sadly. "Maybe he is."

"Giving up old friendships is one test of enlightenment," Grimpen explained. "But there is another test that awaits you. It's a test of courage . . ."

———

71

An hour later, Tash Arranda stood at the edge of a vast pit in the middle of the desert. The sands of Tatooine stretched out in all directions.

What am I doing here? she thought.

Then she pushed the thought away. She knew why she was there. Grimpen had explained it to her: "In order to become truly enlightened, we have to face our fears. All the great monks of the past have gone through a test of courage, and you too must take this step if you are to become enlightened. You must walk in a full circle around the edge of the Great Pit of Carkoon."

Deep in the sand of the Great Pit of Carkoon was where the Sarlacc lived.

The Great Pit of Carkoon wasn't far from Jabba's palace. The sandy pit led down to a wide hole—but it was no ordinary cave or tunnel. The pit was also the mouth of the Sarlacc. The Sarlacc's maw was always open, waiting to devour anyone or anything that came within reach of the tentacles that protruded from its mouth. Row after row of sharp, needlelike teeth stuck out from the sides of the Sarlacc's mouth. Moving around the teeth, the tentacles waited like wriggling tongues, probing for any foolish travelers who came too close.

"There's nothing to it," Tash whispered to herself. "I can do this cruising on sublight engines."

Casually—but carefully—Tash began to walk around the edge of the pit. Once or twice, her footsteps sent a tiny avalanche of sand trickling down the sloping side of the pit and into the Sarlacc's mouth. In response, a thick tentacle would lash out, searching for food, then slither back into the Sarlacc's giant mouth.

Tash was halfway around the circuit and growing very proud of herself. This was a breeze. She could hardly believe Grimpen had made such a big deal of this test. She could hardly believe it was a test at all.

At that moment, a voice nearly shouted in her ear. "Tash, what are you doing?"

It was Zak. He must have followed her. He had snuck up on her during her walk.

These thoughts passed quickly through Tash's mind. Only when she finished thinking them did she realize that she had slipped and fallen to one knee at the edge of the pit.

And only after *that* did she finally understand that she hadn't slipped.

The Sarlacc's tentacle was wrapped around her leg.

CHAPTER 11

The Sarlacc's tentacle was firmly wound around Tash's ankle. One strong pull dragged her a few meters down the side of the pit. Her hands clutched for something to hold on to, but all she grabbed was sand.

"Help!" she cried, her eyes going wide with fear.

Zak lunged forward and grabbed her outstretched hand. He tried to brace himself in the sand, but it was like trying to stand on top of water. His feet just sank into the soft yellow grains.

The Sarlacc pulled again. Tash slid another meter down into the pit, this time dragging Zak with her.

"Do something!" Tash yelled.

"Can you shake free?" he asked.

Tash tried to pull her leg up, but it wouldn't budge. "The Sarlacc's too strong!"

More tentacles started to wriggle upward. The Sarlacc pulled again, dragging Tash closer to its mouth and pulling Zak as well. As he slid down the sandy slope, Zak felt something scratch his stomach. At first he ignored it . . . he had to hold on to Tash! But when the Sarlacc pulled again, the scratch became unbearable. As quickly as he could, Zak reached down to brush the sharp object away. His hand touched something in his pocket. Grabbing it, he pulled the object into view.

He was holding the rusty knife he'd found in the dungeon.

"Hang on, Tash," he urged her. "I've got an idea."

Letting go of her hand, Zak carefully eased himself down beside her. He had to move slowly to keep from slipping too far down the pit.

The Sarlacc's tentacle had wrapped itself twice around Tash's ankle. The brownish-green tentacle looked tough.

"Not as tough as stone," Zak told himself.

He plunged the knife into the Sarlacc's flesh.

Deep beneath them, buried under tons of sand, the Sarlacc roared. The ground trembled, causing little rivers of sand to pour down the slope and into the monster's mouth.

Still, the tentacle held. The Sarlacc refused to give up its meal.

Zak raised the knife and brought it down again. This time the blade sank deep. The tentacle slipped free, taking the knife with it, and slithered back into the Sarlacc's mouth.

Zak and Tash scrambled up the slope until they reached the top of the pit and safety.

Zak climbed to his feet, brushing sand off his clothes as he turned to grin at Tash.

She wasn't smiling.

"You stupid nerfherder!" she yelled.

Zak was stunned.

"You could have gotten me killed!" she fumed.

"I just saved your life!" he protested.

"I didn't need saving until you showed up! I wasn't in any trouble until you made me slip. And by the way, you let the Sarlacc know I was there when you yelled."

Zak tried to argue. "But—"

"Oh, never mind!" she said, stomping off through the sand. "Just stop following me around like a little lost bantha cub!"

Zak made his own way back to Jabba's palace. All he had wanted to do was make sure Tash was safe. Wasn't that the job of a brother? Wasn't that the job of a friend?

Moping through the palace, Zak reached their rooms just as Hoole arrived. "Zak!" the Shi'ido sighed. "Where have you been? Where is Tash?"

" Just . . . around," Zak replied. He'd already made her mad enough. He didn't want to get her in trouble with Uncle Hoole.

Zak let out a deep breath. "Uncle Hoole, can I talk to you?

"I don't understand Tash," Zak said, once they'd seated

themselves in Hoole's room. "We've always been pretty close. Especially after Mom and Dad died. I mean, we get into little fights, but we've always been friends first. Now she treats me like I'm a little kid. It's like she doesn't want to be friends anymore."

Zak felt his face redden. He even *felt* like a little kid saying it.

Hoole's face softened more than Zak had ever seen. The hard lines vanished. Although they'd been together for almost a year now, Zak and Hoole had never had a serious talk.

"Zak," Hoole said gently. "You know I do not have much experience as a parent, or even an uncle. I have always been too busy with my research. So it would be wrong for me to try to sound like a parent now.

"But," he continued, "I think I can help you by telling you what I have noticed as an anthropologist. Humans of Tash's age need to feel grown up. They want to find new friends and new ways to have fun. They change."

Hoole pointed at Zak, then at himself. "I have always found it very strange, the changes humans go through during their lives. We Shi'ido do not do that. Our personalities never change. Humans never change their shape, but their personalities are always changing—sometimes happy, sometimes sad, always finding new interests. Shi'ido, however, change shape all the time, but our personalities remain the same from the day we are born. That is what makes us what we are."

Zak was amazed. Hoole had never spoken to him about anything this personal.

Hoole continued. "But there is an old saying among the Shi'ido: 'No matter how many times we change our shape, we always look like ourselves to those who know us.' It means that whatever shape I choose, my true friends will recognize me."

He put a hand on Zak's shoulder. "What is true for my appearance is true for Tash's personality. I am sure that if you look closely, you will find the Tash you always knew."

Zak could hardly believe his ears. Hoole had always tried to protect his niece and nephew—several times he'd even risked his own life to save theirs. But Zak always thought Hoole was doing what he *had* to do, not what he wanted to do.

Realizing that Hoole really did care for him, Zak took his words to heart. Maybe Hoole was right about Tash. And if he was right, then their friendship could last, whatever Tash was going through.

Excusing himself, Zak went to look for his sister. He had a feeling he knew where to find her.

He caught up with her in the monks' tunnels.

"Hey," he said.

"Hey," she replied.

"I thought you'd be with Grimpen," he said, trying not to sound annoyed.

She shrugged. "I can't find him. I guess he's off meditating somewhere."

Zak took a deep breath. "Look, Tash. I want to apologize for getting on your nerves. I know you want to do other things, without me. It's just hard. You've always been my best friend—even if you *are* my sister."

They both laughed.

"Anyway," he continued, "it's kind of hard for me to sit back and watch you go off somewhere else. But if it's what you want, I can get used to it, I guess."

Tash nodded. "I'm sorry for calling you names before." Then she smiled. "You know, I should be mad at you."

"Why?" Zak asked.

"Because here I am trying to be so mature, and you come along acting more like a grown-up than me!"

Now they really laughed—the way neither of them had laughed in many months.

When he caught his breath, Zak said, "Just promise me that no matter how old we get, we'll still be friends."

"You bet," his sister answered. "We're family, Zak. We can get through anything."

Together, they turned to go.

Together, they froze in sheer terror.

Together, they realized that they were surrounded by brain spiders.

CHAPTER 12

A dozen brain spiders shuffled forward, crowding the hallway. Their metal forelegs rose up, waving in the air, snatching at Zak and Tash.

The two Arrandas leaped backward, and the brain spiders charged.

"I think we can outrun them!" Zak said.

"Why should we run?" Tash asked. "They're just B'omarr monks. I mean, the *brains* of B'omarr monks. They're enlightened, remember? They're not going to hurt us. They're friendly. Watch."

She started in the direction of Grimpen's cell. But a brain spider leaped into her path, its front legs slashing. Zak grabbed his sister's shirt and pulled her back just in time.

"If that's friendly," Zak said, "I'd hate to see them get upset."

Tash cast a confused look at the brain spiders. "I don't get it," she said to the brain inside the mechanical creature. "I thought you were supposed to be— Hey!"

The spider had slashed at her again, nearly slicing a gash in the front of her shirt. "Zak, maybe you're right."

"Come on!" he replied. He and Tash turned and sprinted down the hallway, hoping to put distance between themselves and the mechanical monsters.

Ahead, three shapes with spindly legs scuttled from around a corner.

More brain spiders.

"This way!" Tash suggested, turning down another corridor.

"Do you know where you're going?" Zak gasped between breaths.

"No," Tash panted in reply, "but I'll take any place where those things aren't!"

But the brain spiders seemed to be everywhere. They scurried on their giant legs to cut off every exit. They scuttled down hallways, trying to trap the two Arrandas. The spiders had spent far more time in the tunnels than Zak and Tash. They knew every inch of the underground complex.

There was no escape.

Twice, Zak and Tash passed small groups of B'omarr monks. Each time, Zak and Tash begged them for help, pleading for them to make the brain spiders stop.

The monks ignored them.

"They won't act," Tash gasped. "Grimpen told me that they just don't care about the everyday world. It's like we don't exist to them."

The monks even ignored the brain spiders that scurried into their midst, forcing Zak and Tash to run once more.

No escape.

The Arrandas managed to evade the mechanical spiders for a few more minutes, but finally, they made a wrong turn. They faced a stone wall.

"Dead end," Zak groaned.

"Let's go back," Tash urged.

They turned, but it was too late.

The hallway behind them was filled with brain spiders.

Click-click-click!

A dozen sets of metal legs scraped the tile as they charged forward. Zak and Tash tensed, expecting to be torn to ribbons.

At the last moment, a blur of grayish brown appeared in the corridor. Whatever it was, it moved fast, and it was so tall its head nearly scraped the ceiling of the tunnel. When it finally slowed enough to be seen clearly, Zak and Tash were staring at the last thing they expected to see in the tunnels beneath the desert planet. It was a tauntaun—a giant snow lizard, a creature that could not have survived for more than few minutes on the surface of Tatooine.

The tauntaun crashed into the brain spiders, knocking the legs out from under them with huge swipes of its powerful tail. When the brain spiders continued to press in, the tauntaun suddenly shape-shifted into a thick, muscled humanoid called a Gank. The broad-shouldered Gank lifted the spiders and tossed them against the walls.

The brain spiders retreated. In moments, the hallway was clear.

The Gank turned to look at Zak and Tash. Its skin crawled across its bones, and a moment later it had changed into the shape of a Shi'ido.

"It is a good thing I came to look for you," Hoole said. "I did not think brain spiders acted in that fashion."

"I told you one of them chased me," Zak said.

"Are either of you hurt?" Hoole asked.

Both humans held out their hands and arms to show that they hadn't been cut. "They never really touched us," Tash explained. "It was more like they were herding us somewhere. They were trying to trap us."

"Intriguing," Hoole said. "But it does not matter. We won't be here much longer."

"Did you finish translating those B'omarr documents?" Tash asked.

Hoole shook his head. "Not completely. But I have decided not to accept Jabba's offer. I simply cannot take on a new identity."

Zak knew the reason, but Tash asked, "Why not?"

Hoole explained, "To a Shi'ido like me, identity is everything. I must always remember who I am. Otherwise, with all the shape-changing I do, I am in danger of forgetting who I really am."

"You mean, if you shape-shifted into a Gank, you might forget you weren't *really* a Gank?" Tash asked.

"Exactly." The Shi'ido suddenly morphed with such blinding speed that Tash and Zak caught only glimpses of wings, and fur, and claws, and tails, and beaks, and teeth in a blur of motion. For a moment, Hoole paused, settling on the form of a vornskr, a furry four-legged predator with a poison tail. The fierce creature nipped at Zak and Tash, then changed shape again. When the morphing stopped, Hoole stood before them. "It's important always to remember exactly who you are."

"So we're leaving now?" Tash asked. "But . . . I don't think I'm ready."

"Not ready?" Zak replied in disbelief. "After what just happened?"

"Well, it's not like I want to see brain spiders again, but Grimpen was teaching me so much. I can't leave without saying good-bye."

Hoole considered. "Very well. It is too late to leave tonight anyway. Jabba would be insulted if I didn't say good-bye properly. But I want to make sure nothing else happens to you, Tash."

"I'll be safe," she explained. "The tunnel to Grimpen's meditation chamber is just down that way, and there's a bed of hot coals that the brain spiders can't cross."

"Yes, they can," Zak scoffed, remembering Hoole's comment about the lume rocks. "Remind me to tell you about those so-called hot coals sometime. They wouldn't stop a brain spider for a second.''

Tash shrugged. ''Well, whether they can or can't, I know that they *don't* cross it. They absolutely refuse. So I'll be safe.''

She hurried down the tunnel, with Hoole watching until she was out of sight. He seemed about to change his mind and go after her, when a loud noise drifted down the tunnels. Hoole and Zak heard music and cheering. Something big was happening in Jabba's audience chamber.

Glancing back at Tash, Hoole turned up the hall to investigate.

They reached the audience chamber a few minutes later to find all of Jabba's henchmen gathered around his throne, accompanied by the Imperial officer Commander Fuzzel and a squad of stormtroopers.

Fuzzel shouted over the noise, ''Jabba! You promised me the criminal! What are we waiting for?''

Jabba blinked his huge eyes. ''Patience, Commander, patience. There is merely a short delay in fetching the body. It will arrive any moment now.''

The stormtroopers looked around nervously. They were uncomfortable being surrounded by so many gangsters. As Hoole and Zak watched, Jabba kept them waiting for nearly a quarter of an hour longer. Just as Zak was starting to grow bored, a murmur swept through the crowd.

Bib Fortuna pushed his way through the mob, guiding a

small hoversled. On the hoversled lay a body wrapped in sheets.

Jabba boomed, "As I promised you, Commander Fuzzel, I have delivered the body of the galaxy's most wanted killer. Here is all that remains of Karkas!"

The mob cackled and cheered. Fuzzel stepped forward and pulled back the sheet, revealing a massive head with one crushed eye.

"This is Karkas, all right," Fuzzel said, shaking his head. "That makes five criminals you've turned in this month. You've started up a whole new line of work, Jabba."

"Indeed I have," the Hutt gurgled.

At the edge of the crowd, Zak whispered to Hoole, "I don't get it. When I saw Jabba talking with Karkas yesterday, they were the best of friends. Jabba even promised to help him escape from the Imperials."

"Never trust the promise of a Hutt," Hoole whispered back. "Especially when that Hutt is Jabba."

As the cheering died down, Commander Fuzzel asked, "Just one question, Jabba. What happened to his head?"

"What?" the crime lord rumbled.

Commander Fuzzel pointed down at the body of Karkas. "What happened to his head?"

The Hutt sputtered, "Karkas had one crushed eye. Everyone knows that. He's had it for years."

"Not that," the Imperial said. "This!"

He pointed down to a long scar on the side of the killer's

head. It looked as if someone had slashed him with a vibroblade, except that the cut was very thin and clean.

Jabba shrugged his thick, meaty shoulders. "Karkas must have sustained some injuries when my men took him down. Nothing to worry about. Now, about my money?"

Fuzzel replied, "Yes, yes, you'll get the reward. But I'll tell you this," the Imperial officer added as his men carted the body away, "Karkas is lucky you found him first. If I'd gotten my hands on him, I'd have given him a lot worse than a cut on the back of the skull!"

Jabba's henchmen howled with laughter at the thought of this fat Imperial official trying to take down a killer like Karkas.

"Come along, Zak," Hoole said, "this is not the time to speak with Jabba. I'll say good-bye in the morning. Let's make sure Tash is all right."

Returning to their rooms, Zak saw that his door was open. Tash was inside, stuffing her few belongings into her pack.

"Wouldn't you know it," Zak said. "We don't leave till morning and you're already packed!"

Tash hardly looked at him. "Yeah. Just like me."

Zak shrugged. "I'm not going to pack until later. You want to do something?"

"No," Tash replied.

"Come on," he urged. "We can even do something you want to do. Something grown up, like reading in the monks' library."

Tash snorted. "Why in the name of all the black holes in the galaxy would I wanna hang out with a bunch of frag-eating monks?"

Zak's jaw dropped. "What?"

Tash paused. "Um . . . nothing. Just mind your own business, kid."

" 'Kid'?" Zak snapped. "Why are you back to calling me *kid* again?" He stepped closer to her and looked over her shoulder. "Are you feeling all right?"

"Sure I am," Tash muttered. "Now, get your nose outta my business."

Zak wrinkled his brow. "Why are you talking so funny? Hey, I thought we just made friends again. Why don't you look at me?"

He grabbed her arm.

Tash's reaction was sudden and violent. She whirled around, grabbed Zak by the collar of his tunic, and drove him backward, slamming him against the wall.

"Listen, I ain't got no friends," Tash growled. "Whatever I said before, I was just being nice. I didn't mean it. And if you ever touch me again, I'll eat you for breakfast."

CHAPTER

That night, Zak lay on his bed, drifting in and out of sleep.

He and Tash had not said a word to each other after her outburst, and soon after that Tash had muttered something about feeling like a herd of banthas were stomping through her head. She had crawled into bed and fallen into a dead sleep.

Zak had lain awake for several hours, until a fitful sleep took him. But still his mind replayed the earlier scene over and over. Why had Tash acted like that?

She's been acting strange for days, he reminded himself.

But not like this. Not violent.

She's just going through changes, he replied to his doubts.

Well, if these are the changes, I don't like them.

Remember what Uncle Hoole said. Look for the real Tash. She's in there somewhere.

Zak thought about it, but he couldn't find anything. The Tash he knew was nothing like this one.

The sheets on the bed across the room suddenly billowed up. Zak froze. Tash sat up and stared at him for a moment, as though making sure he was asleep. Zak did his best to breathe regularly, the way a sleeping person did.

Tash got out of bed and quietly pulled on her flight suit. Then, a moment later, she slipped out the door.

What is she doing?

As quickly and quietly as he could, Zak followed her.

Jabba's palace was as quiet as a graveyard. Zak walked on tiptoes as he trailed his sister, who hurried through the many halls of the fortress. She soon reached a section of the palace where neither she nor Zak had been, yet she seemed to know it well. Without missing a step, she went straight through a door that led into an enormous docking bay. On one side of the chamber sat an enormous sail barge, a floating yacht that Jabba used to cruise the desert sand. Beside it, Jabba's hirelings had parked rows of smaller landspeeders and hovercraft. In one corner, in a stall, two dewbacks shuffled. They snorted wearily as they heard people approach. It was far too late to be ridden.

Tash walked straight to one of the landspeeders, hopped inside, and started the repulsor engines.

She's stealing a speeder! Zak was stunned.

A moment later, Tash guided the speeder toward the exit doors, which slid back.

"Tash, wait!" Zak suddenly yelled. "Where are you going?"

She didn't hear him. His voice was drowned out by the whine of the speeder as it roared away.

Zak thought about going back to get Uncle Hoole. But if he did, he would lose Tash's trail. Instead, he ran his eyes over the speeders parked in the docking bay. He didn't know how to fly any of them.

"Now's a good time to learn," he said, hopping into the driver's seat of the nearest speeder.

How hard can it be? he thought as he powered up the small hovercar. He was an expert on his skimboard, and once, with Tash's help, he'd even flown Han Solo's *Millennium Falcon*. Besides, he was no stranger to machines like this—he could take apart this speeder's engine and put it back together in a flash.

Zak pointed the speeder toward the door and hit the accelerator.

The speeder took off. In the wrong direction.

The back of the speeder slammed against the docking-bay wall, making enough noise to wake the dead—which was what Zak would be if Jabba's thugs caught him stealing a vehicle.

"Let's try that again," he grumbled. Flipping a switch, he touched the accelerator. This time, the speeder glided smoothly toward the open door.

Once he was out in the clear desert air, Zak could see the lights of Tash's speeder twinkling like one of the many stars overhead. But she had a huge lead on him, and she'd soon be out of sight.

That's okay, Zak thought. *I know where she's headed. Tash may spend more time studying maps and reading books, but if I remember right, there's only one town in the direction she's going.*

That town was Mos Eisley.

Zak spent the first part of his journey enjoying the power and speed of the landspeeder. It was even more exciting than riding his skimboard. "I could get used to this," he told himself, smiling. Soon, however, he was shivering. As hot as Tatooine was during the day, at night the desert was cold.

By the time Zak glided into the town, even Mos Eisley was asleep. The streets were deserted. All but the most popular cantinas were closed.

Parking the speeder, Zak jumped out and looked around. He had no idea where to begin. Mos Eisley was a big place, and Tash must have arrived long before he did. She could be long gone by now.

But she wasn't. Zak spotted her landspeeder parked near a low, single-story cantina. A hum of voices came from within, accompanied by the slow notes of a tired band playing songs late into the night.

Zak stopped at the doorway. They probably wouldn't let him in . . . and he wasn't sure he wanted to go in anyway.

The idea of entering a Mos Eisley cantina this late at night was about as appealing as the idea of playing tag with a rancor.

Zak was about to turn back when a startled cry reached his ears. It had come from outside the cantina, around the corner.

Creeping forward, Zak heard his sister's voice speak in angry tones: "I hear you were dying to find me. Well, here I am!"

The cry was followed by a sharp *crack!* and someone cried, "N-No! No!"

The cries faded into silence.

Zak ran to the corner and peeked around. He was looking down an alleyway next to the cantina. In the gloom, he could just make out the figure of Tash standing over a large pile of something on the ground. At least, he *thought* it was Tash. Even with so many stars shining, he couldn't be sure it was her. She stooped down over the object on the ground for a moment, then stood up and hurried away.

As soon as she was gone, Zak moved forward to investigate.

He reached the pile and nearly tripped over it. It was much bigger than he thought. In fact, it wasn't a pile at all. It was a body!

Zak recognized the face. It belonged to the Imperial officer, Commander Fuzzel. He was dead. Bending closer, Zak saw something on the dead man's forehead.

The letter *K* had been carved into his skull.

CHAPTER 14

"Help! Murder!"

Zak's cry drifted over the rooftops of Mos Eisley.

Hardly anyone responded. A few heads poked out of windows. Some yelled, "Shut up!" No one bothered to come outside. This was Mos Eisley. Nighttime cries for help were all too common.

"These people are worse than the B'omarr monks!" Zak spat. "These people are just—"

He didn't know what they were. He'd have to ask Tash for the right word.

"Tash," he wondered aloud. "What's going on?"

By the time Zak left the alley, the speeder was gone. Tash must have doubled back or gone through the cantina to reach the front of the building.

Zak thought of the letter *K* cut into Fuzzel's forehead.

That was the mark Karkas left on all his victims. But Karkas was dead—Zak had seen the body with his own eyes.

Stranger still, what had Tash been doing standing over the corpse?

There were only two possible answers. Either Tash had found the body, or Tash had killed Fuzzel. Zak knew the second choice couldn't be true. But why had Tash stolen a landspeeder and come all the way to Mos Eisley?

There was only one way to find out.

By the time Zak guided his landspeeder back to Jabba's palace, the twin suns of Tatooine were already boiling over the horizon.

By now the guards recognized him, and Zak was allowed back into the palace. He went straight to his quarters. Quietly looking into Hoole's room, he saw that his uncle had just risen. Tiptoeing back into his own room, he saw that Tash, too, was awake. She looked a little bleary-eyed, but there was nothing else to suggest that she'd been out most of the night.

Zak got straight to the point. "What were you doing in Mos Eisley?"

Tash looked at him innocently. "What are you talking about?"

"I'm talking about your trip into town!" Zak retorted. "Not to mention the fact that you took a landspeeder without permission, and that you walked away from a dead body!"

For a fraction of a second, Tash looked surprised. "You've got a black hole in your brain. I've been here all night."

Zak snorted. "Come on, Tash, you can tell me. I'll bet this was another one of Grimpen's B'omarr tests. But even you should have called it off when you saw that Commander Fuzzel had been killed."

Tash's glare was like the blast of a turbolaser. "I told you," she growled in an eerily low voice, "I was here all night."

Hoole glided into the room. "We will leave shortly," he said, then noticed the strange looks passing between Tash and Zak.

"Everything's fine," Tash said. "I'll be right back."

Zak waited until she had left the room. "Uncle Hoole, Tash is acting really weird again."

"I thought we had already discussed that," Hoole said flatly.

"No, I mean she's acting *really* strange. Wait till I tell you—"

"Forgive me, Zak. I do want to hear what you have to say," the Shi'ido said, "but I think it is wise to leave here as soon as possible. Once we are safely off Tatooine, then we can deal with Tash's behavior. Until then, we should make it our primary goal to leave Jabba's palace as soon as possible. I am going to pay my respects to Jabba. Please be ready when I return."

When Hoole left, Zak found himself standing alone in

his quarters. He looked at his pack sitting at the foot of his bed.

"You'll have to pit wait," he muttered as he took off after Tash.

As before, Tash was easy to follow. She strode through Jabba's palace with ease. She obviously wasn't expecting anyone to follow, because she never once looked back.

Her course took her past Jabba's throne room and down a wide corridor. This hallway was decorated with holo-pictures and statues—all of Jabba himself.

This must be Jabba's private quarters, Zak guessed. *Only a Hutt would have an ego big enough to cover his walls with pictures of himself*

At the end of the hall stood a high, wide door. Four Gamorrean guards sat on either side, snorting and snuffling at each other. As Tash approached, one of the guards jumped up and waddled over to a control panel. The door slid open, and Tash walked calmly inside.

Now what? Zak wondered.

Boldly, he strode up to the door as well. This time all four Gamorreans jumped to their feet. They brandished their vibro-axes and snorted angrily in his direction. One of the guards jabbed at him with an ax.

"All right!" Zak said, jumping back. "I get the hint."

He hurried away before he could attract any more attention.

As he retreated down the hallway, Zak tried to put together the pieces of this strange puzzle. But there were too many. First there was Beidlo's idea that the B'omarr monks were performing unnecessary brain transfers. Then Beidlo had said he'd been mistaken. Then there was the attack of the brain spiders. That was almost as strange as Jabba, who first promised to help the killer Karkas and then turned his dead body in to Commander Fuzzel. Then, that very night, Fuzzel was murdered—apparently by Karkas, who was supposed to be dead.

Click-click-click . . .

Zak's mind reeled. "The only thing that's stayed the same," he muttered, "is that Tash has been acting weird. But not *this* weird!"

Click-click-click . . .

Zak was so lost in thought that he didn't see the brain spider until it was on top of him. When those spidery legs came into view, he leaped backward, bumping into something hard and sharp.

There was another brain spider behind him.

"Oh, no!" Zak gasped. He closed his eyes so he wouldn't see the deathblow coming.

But the spiders didn't attack him. Instead, they pushed forward gently on their durasteel legs, nudging him.

"Hey, watch it," he said, looking at the brains inside each droid. Each brain looked like a round pile of thick noodles.

The spiders pushed again, and again, until Zak realized that they weren't trying to hurt him. They were pushing him toward one side of the corridor. They were herding him, just as Tash had said before.

Not wanting to feel those sharp legs on his skin, Zak went in the direction the brain spiders were shoving him. He saw a small hatch set into the wall—the kind of small door that maintenance workers use to get into tight spaces in a building. One of the spiders scurried forward and tapped at the door with a foreleg.

"You want me to open it?" Zak asked.

He deactivated the lock, and the automatic door popped open. A sharp poke in the back from one of the spiders made him jump and sent him stumbling into the maintenance hall.

The floor was covered with sand, like a mini-desert—probably the leftovers from years of sweeping out Jabba's hallways.

The spiders crept forward, forcing Zak to go farther down the sandy hallway.

"Look, I don't know what you want," Zak said. He didn't know if the brains inside the spiders could hear or understand him, but it was worth a try. "I thought you B'omarr monk brains were supposed to contemplate the universe or something—not pick on Jabba's guests."

"Hoohoohoohoo!"

Zak blinked. Were the brain spiders laughing?

"Hooohoo!"

No, that laughter belonged to Jabba the Hutt! It was coming from overhead. Zak looked up. About two meters up the wall of the maintenance hall was a vent. The Hutt's deep laughter was trickling through it.

One of the brain spiders moved beneath the vent and lowered itself so that it sat on the floor.

Zak quickly figured out what it wanted. "You're offering me a boost?"

He stepped onto the spider-droid's back, careful to avoid the glass jar containing the wrinkled brain. With a whine of servos, the brain spider rose to its normal height, lifting Zak up to the vent.

Zak peeked through the tiny metal grate.

He was looking inside Jabba's private chambers! What he saw amazed him.

Jabba the Hutt reclined on a wide couch, rolls of fat rising and falling across the length of his body.

Nearby sat Tash. She had her feet up on a table covered with strange and exotic foods. As Zak watched, she reached into a bowl full of live eels. Fishing one out, she opened her mouth wide and dropped the wriggling creature in. The eel's tail flapped once as it struggled to escape; then Tash swallowed it with a contented sigh.

Jabba growled, "I notice that the credits still have not been sent to my account."

Tash nodded. "That's right, Jabba. You're not getting your money until we fix this problem."

"I already explained," the crime lord said as he smacked his lips. "Someone freed the prisoner we had reserved for you. We had no other choice, especially with the Imperials approaching.''

''Yeah, but now I'm stuck with this!'' Tash said, pointing at herself.

''Look on the bright side,'' the Hutt gurgled in amusement, ''no Imperials will ever stop you again.''

''Very funny,'' Tash snapped back. ''But I'm telling you I want this fixed, and fixed now!''

Jabba checked a small datascreen near his couch. ''Ah, just the message I was waiting for. Don't worry, my friend. I have the perfect solution. Right this way.''

The Hutt slithered off his couch and Tash stood up. Together, they moved out of Zak's view. A moment later he heard a door open and close.

Jumping down from the brain spider's back, Zak rubbed his forehead. He was getting a headache. ''What in all the galaxy is going on here?''

The brain spider that had lifted him now extended one of its legs. The leg made a few slow, small movements in the sand. But the motion was clumsy—the spider's legs weren't made for such delicate action.

After several tries, the spider finally succeeded in moving its leg the way it wanted. Finally, when it was satisfied, the brain spider stepped back and let Zak see its work.

Zak's heart froze and his blood went cold in his veins.

In a jagged, uneven style, the brain spider had written two words.

I'M TASH.

CHAPTER 15

I'M TASH.

The words lay in the sand. The brain spider danced back and forth on its spindly legs.

"I—I don't understand," Zak stammered. He had just seen Tash talking with Jabba!

No.

He had seen Tash's *body* talking with Jabba.

Zak looked at the brain spider. He looked at the brain inside the jar.

Tash's brain.

It all made sense to him now. The B'omarr monks had removed Tash's brain and put it into a brain spider. Then they had put someone else's brain into her body!

Zak recalled the letter *K* on Fuzzel's skull.

It was Karkas.

Jabba hadn't killed him. He had put the killer's brain in Tash's head, then given Karkas's body to the Imperials.

"Of course," Zak said in a frightened whisper. "That's been Jabba's plan all along. He hasn't been turning in wanted criminals to the authorities. He's been giving them new bodies! The criminals pay Jabba and leave Tatooine with completely new identities. Jabba gives their old bodies to the Imperials and collects even more credits!"

It all made sense. Beidlo had been right. The monks *were* performing too many operations! And they weren't always using other monks. That was why that prisoner had been held in Jabba's dungeon. Jabba was using anyone he could find to provide bodies for his customers!

Zak felt a sudden pang of guilt. He remembered the words Jabba had just spoken: *Someone freed the prisoner we had reserved for you.*

Zak had freed the prisoner. And because he had let the captive go, Jabba had needed another body for Karkas.

Tash's body.

"I'm sorry, Tash," Zak said to the brain spider. "It's my fault."

The brain spider hopped up and down excitedly as if to say, *Don't apologize. Do something!*

Another brain spider shuffled forward, bobbing up and down on its mechanical legs. Staring at the other brain, Zak had a strange feeling he knew who it was.

"Beidlo," he whispered. "You're in there."

The brain spider bobbed rapidly.

Zak held back angry tears. Jabba had given the young monk's body to some other criminal. That was why the fake Beidlo had denied his story in front of Uncle Hoole.

"Uncle Hoole," Zak said. "I've got to tell Uncle Hoole!"

Zak knew he could easily outrun the brain spiders, so he said, "Don't follow me. Meet me at the entrance to the B'omarr tunnels."

He hurried out of the maintenance hall and into the main corridor. He didn't care who saw him sprint full speed through the palace and back to his quarters.

But their rooms were empty. Hoole had not returned.

Turning back, Zak sprinted again, this time for Jabba's throne room. It, too, was empty.

Where now? Zak thought.

There were only the B'omarr monks left, but Zak couldn't go to them because they were performing the operations for Jabba. Getting help from the monks was out of the question.

Or was it?

There was Grimpen. Tash liked him, and Tash's intuitions usually proved reliable. Besides, Grimpen had been different from the other monks—less dark and brooding. Beidlo had mentioned something about asking for his help, but obviously he had been captured before he got the chance.

There was no one else to turn to. Zak took a deep breath and raced off again.

By the time he reached the tunnels, Tash and Beidlo—inside their brain spiders—were there. Zak had lost his fear of the brain spiders. He was sure now that the spiders that had seemed to attack him earlier had just been more of Jabba's victims, trying desperately to communicate with someone who might help them.

Zak looked at the globe of gray, wrinkled flesh inside the brain spider's jar and shuddered. He had to remind himself that *that* was his sister. "Tash, I need help. Can you lead me to Grimpen?"

The brain spiders bobbed up and down excitedly, but made no other move.

Zak tried again. "I need to find Grimpen. You've been to his quarters more often than I have. Which way are they?"

The two spiders shuffled from side to side, but then returned to their original spots. Zak scratched his head. Maybe Tash couldn't hear him.

He shrugged. He'd have to find Grimpen on his own.

Tash and Beidlo followed as Zak hurried through the maze of passageways, trying to remember the way to Grimpen's meditation chamber. Finally, he found the long, dark hallway, with the faint glow of the coal bed in the distance.

By now, Zak was so panic-stricken and desperate for help that he didn't notice the brain spiders behind him. If he had looked back, he would have seen them stop. They refused to go farther. Instead, they danced back and forth frantically, trying to get his attention.

But he was running too quickly to notice.

A few more moments brought Zak to the edge of the glowing rocks. He didn't even hesitate.

"Lume rocks," he muttered, remembering what Uncle Hoole had told him. "Not even warm."

He churned up piles of glowing stones as he ran across the bed and reached the other side.

Beyond the bed of lume rocks, Zak found the door to a monk's cell. It opened automatically and Zak stepped inside.

Grimpen sat on a short, wide platform. His face was very calm. He smiled at Zak. "Hello, Zak. I've been expecting you."

"Y-You have?" Zak panted, trying to catch his breath.

Grimpen nodded. "I know why you have come," the monk said distantly. "I know many things."

Zak nodded. "Then Tash must have figured out a way to tell you, too. Did she warn you?"

"Warn me?" Grimpen replied. "Tash has warned me of nothing."

"What is it then?" Zak gasped. "Part of your enlightenment? Is that how you know about Jabba's brain transfers?"

Grimpen chuckled. "Of course not. I know about Jabba's brain transfers because I'm the one who's been performing them."

CHAPTER

16

Zak backed away in horror, but Grimpen was faster. The monk lunged forward and grabbed Zak's arm. His grip felt as strong as a Wookiee's.

"Now, now, there's no need to be afraid," Grimpen scolded. "Soon enough Jabba will have another customer in need of a new identity, and then we'll have use for you. You should consider it an honor." Grimpen laughed. "Kept alive inside a spider, your brain will have centuries to contemplate the universe."

Keeping a viselike grip on Zak's arm, Grimpen dragged him out of the meditation chamber. "Come along. I have an appointment. I think you'll want to be there."

Grimpen stomped over the lume rocks. "I suppose you know about these," he said with a laugh. "You'd be amazed how often that trick works. It gets my victims to think they really are enlightened. I just throw a few such simple tests their way, and when they pass, they think they're ready to solve the mysteries of the universe!''

Zak winced at the pain in his arm. "That Sarlacc test wasn't so easy."

"Of course it was," Grimpen mocked. "The Sarlacc wouldn't have bothered Tash if you hadn't been so clumsy. Anyway, your sister was already convinced she was going to be the greatest thinker in the galaxy. That only made things easier for me. Half the time, my subjects are so convinced that they're enlightened, they don't even put up a struggle when I scoop out their brains!''

Grimpen strode through the main halls of the B'omarr monks, dragging Zak with him. The brain spiders—Tash and Beidlo—jabbed at Grimpen with their metal legs, but the monk brushed them aside.

They reached the portal Zak had seen on his first day. Beyond it lay the Great Room of the Enlightened, where they'd stumbled on the monks performing the brain operation. The walls were covered with shelves, and the shelves were filled with jars, and the jars were filled with brains floating in chemical soup.

This time Zak got a closer look at the table in the center of the room. There were leather restraints attached to each corner. Beside the table sat a tray of medical instruments. Some of them were modern tools—laser-needles and vibroscalpels. But there were older, more wicked-looking tools as well—blades with jagged edges, and a heavy saw.

"For sawing through the skull," Grimpen explained. "Very difficult."

Keeping one hand on Zak, Grimpen pulled a handheld vidscreen from his robes. As it powered up, Zak could see the fleshy face of Jabba the Hutt on the small monitor.

"Jabba," Grimpen said, "I'm in the Great Room. I'm ready to operate."

"Your patient is on his way," the crime lord boomed over the speaker. "The sooner the better. I want Karkas's credits!"

"I have the Arranda child as well," Grimpen added.

"Good!" Jabba crowed. "I'm sure we can make use of his body. But only after we're done with the other victim I'm sending you."

Zak looked around desperately. There was nothing in the room to use as a weapon. He wished for the rusty knife, but he'd left it sticking in the Sarlacc's tentacle.

Footsteps approached the Great Room.

"Ah, here comes our patient now," Grimpen said.

Everything's going to be all right, Zak told himself, staring at the floor. *Things have been worse. Uncle Hoole is still out there somewhere, and he always appears at the last minute. He always saves us.*

"Welcome," Grimpen said.

Zak looked up. Tash had entered the room, accompanied

by two Gamorrean guards. Not Tash, Zak reminded himself, but the killer Karkas in Tash's body. She—he—was guiding a small hoversled.

Come on, Uncle Hoole, Zak thought. *Where are you?*

As the hoversled approached, Zak saw that someone lay on it.

That someone was Hoole.

CHAPTER 17

Hoole lay unconscious on the hoversled. He was the other victim Jabba had mentioned. Zak moaned. For the first time, he realized that he might have failed. He would end up trapped inside a jar until the end of time.

"They're here," Grimpen said. "I'll call you again after the operation. Grimpen out." He snapped the vidscreen shut.

Grimpen nodded to Karkas. "Did you have any trouble?"

Karkas, behind Tash's face, smirked. "Not much. This girl's body is weaker than a nerf cub. But the Shi'ido wasn't expecting to get brained by his own niece." Karkas laughed with Tash's clear laugh. "Get it? *Brained!*"

"Humorous," Grimpen said dryly. "Are you ready?"

Karkas snorted. "I can't wait to get out of this stupid

body." The criminal leered over Hoole's unconscious figure. "This one will do much better. And the best part of it is, no one will ever suspect that Karkas the killer is hiding inside a Shi'ido."

Zak shuddered. They were going to perform another brain transfer and put Karkas's brain inside Hoole's body. Would that mean that Karkas would have Hoole's shape-changing power? Did the Shi'ido ability come from the body or from the mind? Hoole had never told them.

"Here, watch the boy," Grimpen said. He shoved Zak toward Karkas. The killer grabbed Zak with Tash's hand, drawing a blaster with the other.

For a second, Zak considered fighting back. Karkas was a killer who had terrorized the galaxy, but right now he was trapped in the body of a thirteen-year-old girl. Zak wasn't quite as tall as Tash, but he was strong, and he was more of an athlete than Tash was. He was sure he could beat her.

But as soon as Karkas clutched him, Zak abandoned the idea. The hand on his arm was Tash's hand, but it wasn't. They were her fingers, but the grip felt nothing like hers. It was hard and mean. Zak could tell that if he made any sudden moves, Karkas would kill him without a thought.

Besides, even if he could wrestle free, he would still have to deal with Grimpen and the two Gamorrean guards.

The monk positioned the hoversled next to the table. With the help of Jabba's Gamorreans, he slid Hoole onto the operating table and then bound his hands and feet with the leather straps.

"One cannot be too careful," he observed as he began to sort through the trayful of instruments. "I think I'll do this the old-fashioned way," he said, casually picking up the skull saw.

"No!" Zak yelled.

Grimpen only smiled. He lowered the saw until its sharp teeth rested on Hoole's forehead.

Hoole's eyes flew open.

One of the Gamorreans snorted.

"He's awake!" Karkas yelled.

"It's of no concern," Grimpen assured him. "I've had several patients wake during the brain transfer. He's securely tied down."

Karkas lunged forward, aiming the blaster. "No, you idiot. He's a Shi—*aahh!*"

His warning turned into a cry of surprise as Zak tripped him up. Tash's body sprawled onto the stone floor of the Great Room of the Enlightened.

On the table, Hoole tugged once at his restraints and then closed his eyes. His entire body shifted and collapsed on itself, morphing into the form of a Circapousian water snake. The snake slithered easily out of the straps and dropped onto the floor as the Gamorreans squealed and jumped back in surprise. They recovered quickly, and both guards chopped down with their axes. But Hoole changed shape again, this time becoming a tall, thin-bodied Duro. The axes passed harmlessly on either side of him and struck the floor in a shower of sparks.

113

A few meters away, Zak dove on top of Karkas, struggling to gain control of the blaster. He managed to pin down the hand that held the blaster, but he didn't know what to do next. He was fighting his own sister!

Karkas lashed out with a savage elbow that snapped Zak's head backward. For a moment the blaster came free, and Karkas leveled the weapon at Hoole.

"No!" Zak shouted. He punched as hard as he could, hitting the side of Tash's face. The blow made the blaster shot go wide, slamming into the wall and shattering a shelf full of brain jars. Yellow-green chemicals and gray brains oozed down the walls and onto the floor.

Near the shelf, Hoole shifted again. He became a vornskr, leaping forward on all four feet, his poison tail whipping behind him. The vornskr lunged at a Gamorrean, jaws snapping. At the same time, its tail lashed out at the other guard, slashing the guard's snout.

The first guard struck back with his ax, but the vornskr easily dodged away, then snapped the ax handle in half with one bite of its jaws.

Weaponless, the Gamorrean fled in terror. The vornskr turned back to its first opponent, but the guard, stunned by the poison, had already fallen to the ground.

Zak was still on the ground, too. Now he was throwing punches. It was Tash's face he was hitting, but his blows were rattling Karka's brain. The killer blacked out and the blaster dropped from his hand.

Zak's heart was still racing from his fight with Karkas. He scrambled to his feet, aiming the blaster at Grimpen. "Don't move or I'll enlighten you in a whole new way."

Grimpen kept as still as stone.

Hoole, back in his own shape, walked over to Zak's side. Zak said, "I'm so glad you woke up."

Hoole nodded. "I was never really unconscious. I only pretended to let Karkas overpower me. I could not make a move with Jabba's personal army all around."

"You mean, you knew it wasn't Tash?" Zak said, startled.

"Only at the last moment," the Shi'ido confessed. "I took my own advice when I noticed how extremely odd she was acting. I could not find the real Tash in her, so I became suspicious. Of course, I did not know the whole story until Karkas brought me down here." He looked proudly at Zak. "You, however, found out on your own. Excellent work."

"Thanks, Uncle Hoole," Zak said. "For a minute there I thought you were dead. Looks like you've saved us again." He pointed at Grimpen. "But now what?"

"I suggest that we—" Hoole started to say, then stopped.

B'omarr monks were gliding into the room on quiet feet. The first few monks moved quickly to the damaged shelves, gathering up the brains that had burst free of their jars. Carefully, the monks collected the brains in deep pans, pouring liquid over them. But as more monks entered the chamber, they turned toward the intruders. First a few, then a dozen, then twenty, then so many Zak lost count. The brown-robed monks formed a circle around Zak, Hoole, and Grimpen.

They were surrounded.

CHAPTER

18

"What do you want?" Hoole demanded.

One of the monks stepped forward. "This must end. Your presence has caused great disturbance."

"Don't blame us, blame him," Zak said, pointing at Grimpen.

The monk who had spoken bowed his head once in acknowledgment. "He has given our secrets to outsiders. He shall be punished."

"You won't do anything to me," Grimpen snarled. "Jabba will have your heads!"

The monk nodded to some of his brothers. At his silent command, several of the B'omarr surrounded Grimpen.

"What? No!" Grimpen cried. His shouts were suddenly muffled as he vanished behind a curtain of brown robes.

Zak did not see them take the treacherous monk out of the room. Grimpen simply vanished.

The first monk turned back to Hoole and Zak. "Now go," he ordered them.

"Wait." Hoole pointed at the two brain spiders that had been lurking in the shadows. "We need your help. My niece is trapped inside that brain spider. You must return her to her own body."

The monk paused. "For what purpose? In this state she may achieve enlightenment."

The spider droid holding Tash's brain scuttled to and fro frantically. It was easy to see what she was saying: *No, no!*

"She's not a monk," Hoole argued. "She is not prepared for this kind of enlightenment."

The speaker intoned, "The universe moves as it will. We have no interest in undoing what has been done. We do not take interest in the actions of outsiders."

Hoole, however, was not finished with them. He pulled a tube from the pocket of his robe. Popping the cap off the end of the tube, he withdrew a scroll. "Then perhaps you will take an interest in this."

A murmur rippled through the crowd of monks—the loudest noise they had made in all that time. They recognized what Hoole was holding.

It was the scroll Jabba had stolen.

"You value your secrets," Hoole said. "Then let us make a bargain. If you return my niece to her natural state, I will give the scroll back to you. If you refuse, I will spread the contents of this scroll from one end of the galaxy to the other. Everyone will know how you sometimes use tricks to attract students. Worse still, the entire galaxy will know your secrets for brain transference.''

The monks had no choice but to agree. They quickly set to work, preparing Tash's body and making sure her brain was still healthy inside the spider.

"What about Jabba?" Zak considered. "He's up there waiting for a call from Grimpen."

Hoole shrugged. "Then Grimpen shall call him."

The Shi'ido took the mini-vidscreen that Grimpen had left behind and shifted into Grimpen's shape. He activated the vidscreen.

Jabba's face materialized on the monitor. "How did the operation go?"

"Everything has turned out very well," said Hoole in Grimpen's form. "Give me a short time, and I'll be done. I'm sure you'll be surprised at the results. Grimpen out."

EPILOGUE

"Starship *Shroud,* you are cleared for takeoff," said a voice over the loudspeaker.

"Affirmative, traffic control," Hoole replied. "Preparing to launch."

The Shi'ido turned to Zak and Tash. "Are you strapped in?"

"Ready," they both said.

As they waited for takeoff, Zak looked out over the city of Mos Eisley.

"Do you think Beidlo will be all right?" he wondered.

Tash shrugged. "I hope so. His body was gone, so his brain had to stay in the brain spider. But he wasn't like me. He *wanted* to have his brain transferred someday. The monks will help him adjust to his new life."

Zak turned to check on his sister one more time. The monks had done their work well, and Tash looked as if she'd never been through the amazing procedure. The monks were so skilled, in fact, that there weren't even any scars left over from the operation. The only physical proof that she'd been through anything at all was the set of bruises Zak had pounded into her body.

"I wouldn't want to make a brain spider my permanent home, but it wasn't that bad," Tash continued. "I could sort of see and hear through the droid's sensors, but it was all foggy."

She paused.

"Of course, I guess my senses were kind of foggy even before that. Zak, I'm sorry I didn't see through Grimpen's flattery right away. I'm also sorry about . . . about everything. I hope you weren't too mad."

Zak laughed. "I'm over it. Besides, how often does a guy get to pummel his own snobby sister and come out looking like a hero?"

Tash groaned as the ship lifted off and headed into infinite space.

Below Jabba's palace, in the Great Room of the Enlightened, Jabba roared at the row of monks standing before him. He yelled so loudly that the hundreds of brain jars on the walls shook.

"Where is Grimpen?" the Hutt demanded. "Where is Karkas?"

The monks said nothing.

"I could have you all vaporized!" Jabba threatened.

"The universe moves as it will," one of the monks responded.

Jabba fumed. He would not kill them all. He needed them to find Grimpen. Grimpen was the only monk willing to reveal their secrets.

"Someday I'll find him," Jabba declared as he turned and slithered away. "Someday."

The monks watched him depart. Above their heads, on the fourth shelf from the top, in the third jar from the left, one of the brains almost seemed to shudder frantically in its pool of yellow-green chemicals.

I'm here! Grimpen screamed. But he had no mouth to yell with. *Help me!*

No one heard him, except perhaps for a few very enlightened monks. But they ignored him. They knew that Grimpen would remain on his shelf until he became enlightened, or until the end of time.

Whichever came first.

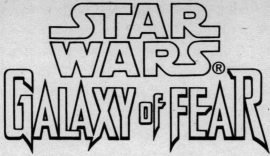

Hoole, Tash, and Zak continue their journeys to the darkest reaches of the galaxy in *The Swarm,* the next book in the Star Wars: Galaxy of Fear series. For a sneak preview, turn the page!

AN EXCERPT FROM

BOOK 8

THE SWARM

Zak and Tash rushed forward to help the officer. Thrawn remained behind, studying the scene with cold efficiency.

Zak and Tash both fell to their knees, trying to brush the swarming drog beetles from the Imperial's body. Some of the beetles landed in the grass and waddled away to investigate other things, but most merely opened their wings and fluttered back toward the body.

"Help us!" Zak called out to Thrawn.

"Don't bother," the Imperial captain replied. "He's dead."

Thrawn was right. The body wasn't moving. The officer's skin was already pale and cold. Zak could see wriggling bulges in his uniform where the beetles had crawled under his clothes.

Something bit Zak. "Ow!" he yelled, leaping back.

Tash looked up. "Zak, what's—ow!" She jumped to her feet, too, sticking her finger in her mouth. "One of those things bit me!"

"Me too," Zak said. He looked at his hand. There was a tiny red mark. "I guess they don't want us interfering with their meal." He shuddered.

Behind them, Captain Thrawn pulled a comlink from his belt and spoke to someone on the other end, probably on board the Star Destroyer orbiting overhead. "This is Captain Thrawn. Order the entire Sikadian Garden sealed. All ships within one thousand kilometers are to be grounded immediately, then searched. Someone has murdered Lieutenant Wolver."

Thrawn moved with lightning-fast efficiency. Tash and Zak watched as, for the next hour, Imperial investigators shuttled down from Thrawn's Star Destroyer to examine the area. A medical team examined the body where it lay. Imperial crewmen cut tree branches and uprooted bushes, using them as brushes to drive the swarming beetles away.

As they did, Vroon seemed to materialize out of nowhere. His wings hummed angrily, and he said, "I must protest! This garden is a protected area. You can't just come in here, tearing up the plants. And the beetles! You must not—''

Thrawn waved him off. ''I will do whatever I must. One of my men has been murdered. The investigation is more important than your bugs.''

But Vroon continued to complain until Thrawn ordered his men to take the caretaker away. At that, Vroon hurried off, complaining as he disappeared down one of the garden's many paths.

Once the drog beetles were removed from the body, the medical examiner found several large wounds.

''What caused the wounds?'' Thrawn demanded.

''Difficult to say,'' the doctor replied. ''I'm not sure if they were made before the beetles did their work, or if the insects crawled into the existing holes and made them wider. But I would say that, if anything, the wounds were made by a very large handweapon, perhaps a vibropike.''

Zak and Tash looked at each other, remembering Sh'shak.

Thrawn spoke through his comlink. ''Thrawn to Star Destroyer *Vengeance*. Begin monitoring all planetary transmissions. It's possible that there is an anti-Imperial group operating on S'krrr. They may have murdered Lieutenant Wolver. Keep me informed.''

Tash and Zak slipped off while Thrawn was giving

orders for the body's removal, and returned to the *Shroud*.

They found Hoole waiting with a frown etched deeply into his face. The interior of the *Shroud* looked like it had been torn apart by Tusken Raiders.

"Zak, Tash, I'm relieved to see you here. Storm-troopers marched through here and searched the *Shroud*. They would not say what they were looking for."

"They were looking for a murderer!" Zak replied.

"We were with Captain Thrawn. We found one of his officers. The man was dead, and there were drog beetles all over him." Tash shuddered.

Zak added, "And you won't believe it. Earlier, we saw—"

He stopped. Sh'shak had suddenly appeared.

"Oh," Zak ended lamely.

"Yes, Zak?" Hoole prodded.

Zak swallowed. "Nothing. It's just that Captain Thrawn thinks there are anti-Imperial agents on the planet."

Sh'shak's wings hummed. "Most interesting. If that is the case, the Imperials may declare a curfew. I must finish some errands before they do so." He bowed to Hoole. "It was a pleasure speaking with you. Good day."

Zak waited until the S'krrr was out of sight. "He's the murderer!"

Hoole blinked. "Nonsense."

"But we saw him practicing with a vibropike!" Zak insisted. "He looked like a killing machine."

"I think Zak may be right, Uncle Hoole," Tash admitted. "Sh'shak told me he was a poet, but after what I saw today . . ."

Hoole shook his head. "Zak, Tash, this is where an understanding of alien cultures can help you. You see, the S'krrr are—"

Hoole's sentence was cut off by the sound of pounding on the ship's hull. Hoole looked outside to find Thrawn's other lieutenant, Tiers, waiting. "You are to come with me," he said to Hoole.

"But I have not done anything," Hoole replied.

"Captain Thrawn is questioning everyone," Lieutenant Tiers declared. He pointed at Zak and Tash. "They can remain behind."

Hoole was gone a long time. Zak and Tash could do nothing but wait impatiently, pacing the corridors of the *Shroud,* tapping their fingers against the powerless computer monitors.

"Do you think Sh'shak did it?" Zak finally asked. "Do you think he's a Rebel?"

"Maybe, to the first question," his sister replied.

"But I doubt it, to the second. Think about the Rebels we've met in the past. Luke Skywalker and Princess Leia, and even Wedge a few months ago. They were willing to fight for what they believed in, but none of them were cold-blooded killers."

"And neither, it seems, am I," said Uncle Hoole, suddenly stepping through the door.

"Uncle Hoole!" the Arrandas shouted together. "You're all right!"

"Indeed," Hoole replied, "although it was touch and go for a while. I make rather a suspicious character these days, it seems. Previously, I could use my credentials as an anthropologist to explain my travels. But now it hardly seems wise to mention my true name, since we're all wanted by the Empire."

Hoole explained that he'd managed to convince the Imperials that he and the two Arrandas were on a cultural field trip. Since he could prove he'd been at the *Shroud* working on the engines all morning, the rest of his story worked.

Tash tried to break in. "Uncle Hoole, there's something we should tell you about Sh'shak . . ."

But Hoole was already heading toward his cabin. "I'm afraid it will have to wait until morning, Tash. I am quite weary from the questions, and I must consider how we can leave this planet safely, and soon."

As he entered his room, he added, "There will be

more questions in the morning. Thrawn has sent most of his men back to his Star Destroyer, but he is determined to find the murderer. We should all get some rest to prepare ourselves for more questioning tomorrow.''

Zak went to his cabin, shoved a pile of clothes, datacards, and his trusty skimboard off the bed, slipped into a sleep suit, and finally fell in a heap on the bunk. He'd gotten up early that morning, and he was tired. Their visit to S'krrr was turning into a nightmare. Now, even if they'd fixed the *Shroud*'s engines, Thrawn could keep them grounded until he found the killer.

Killer! Zak's heart skipped a beat. In all the excitement, he'd forgotten about the shreev he killed. He'd forgotten to kill thirty beetles! Frantically, he tried to remember if the Imperials had killed any while they examined the body. Were the beetles just driven off, or were they crushed? And if some were crushed, how many?

Zak groaned. ''You blew it again, Zak Arranda.''

But then he tried to calm down. Missing one day couldn't be that bad, could it? After all, he could always try to get sixty of the beetles tomorrow.

He nodded. That would do it. He'd simply catch up tomorrow. With that comforting thought, Zak drifted off to sleep.

He woke up hours later in the dark. Something was tickling his ear. He yawned. "Tash, stop it. Go away."

Something tickled his ear again. "Tash, I don't care who you want to spy on now, I'm staying in bed." He opened his eyes.

Tash wasn't there.

Tiny legs scampered across his cheek and scurried up into his hair. Slapping at it, Zak sat up and snapped on his cabin lights.

His bed was covered with drog beetles.

ABOUT THE AUTHOR

John Whitman has written several interactive adventures for *Where in the World Is Carmen Sandiego?,* as well as many Star Wars stories for audio and print. He is an executive editor for Time Warner AudioBooks and lives in Encino, California.

Is the Force with you?

To find out read . . .

CHOOSE YOUR OWN
STAR WARS®
ADVENTURE™

A NEW HOPE

Limited Collector Edition 3-D Hologram Cover!

CHRISTOPHER GOLDEN

LIMITED COLLECTOR'S EDITION

0-553-48651-9

Available March 9, 1998, wherever books are sold.

Join Luke, Princess Leia, and Han Solo and fight against the evil Galactic Empire—only this time *you* control the twists, turns, and outcomes of the most exciting adventure in the galaxy. Will you lead the Rebellion to victory against the Empire? Or side with Darth Vader and betray your friends? The fate of the galaxy is in *your* hands in this interactive novel based on the original *Star Wars* film.

BFYR161